TIC TAC TOE

EMMY ELLIS

ACKNOWLEDGEMENTS

Thank you to the following people for allowing me to use their names as I saw fit:

Zac Ferguson, Susan Burrow, Michele Oberlander, Jambrea Gaff, Erica Orloff, Keith Crow, Claire Billing, Wendy Tynen, Rhiannon Tynen, Roslynn Ernst

PROLOGUE

The chalk. The pavement. The noughts and crosses—that was what they called it, the game. *He* called it tic-tac-toe for…reasons.

He laughed, thinking about the sight they'd see once they found her, that stupid, insipid cow who'd got on his wick in the library. Who did she think she was, eh? He'd only coughed, and she'd come down on him, whisper-shouting, saying if he was noisy one more time, that was it, he'd be banned. That had been the last straw. She'd been needling him about other stuff for too long.

Bitch.

It was open late tonight for some meeting or other, people in a book club discussing the latest fiction that had stormed the charts. Cartoon cover, swirly font. Not his cuppa, but then the sort of thing he read didn't go down well with others, so there you go. Different tastes and all that. He preferred a bit of stabbing and murder himself, the gorier the better.

From his vantage point in the bushes at the back of the car park, he stared over at the one-storey building, with its yellow glow inside from the central lights she'd left on. The group sat in a circle in the middle, yabbering away, each of them with a book in hand, six women and two blokes, and *her*, presiding over them all like some hen-pecking twat. Bet she wouldn't be telling them to *shh*, would she. No, it was fine to make a noise when she said so.

Anger burned, and he swallowed down the nausea it brought on. Fucking hell, who knew he had it in him to do this? He certainly hadn't, not until he'd thought about strangling her or punching her face in, and the need to do it for real had taken root, then his main idea had surfaced. He'd been planning this for weeks now, as well as the others—anyone and everyone who'd naffed him off. He'd get rid of them and be happier for it. Things had happened in his childhood, had shaped his thoughts, the way he behaved. He'd hidden everything inside, but a couple of weeks ago, the memories had popped into his head, taunting him.

He had to do all this to stop them resurfacing.

A check of his watch, the turquoise light a little circle in the darkness, and he counted down the time. The meeting would end at ten and, give or take a few minutes for the club members to sod off, he'd have her all to himself.

He rubbed his hands at that.

He waited. Imagined killing her. Got it straight in his head. He could do this, couldn't he? The moment to walk away was now if he wasn't sure.

Stay. Do it.

The first person came out, got in her car, and drove off. Then a few others did the same, leaving only the blokes. He breathed out in relief when they exited, getting in the same car together and speeding away. Brothers. A bit unnecessary with the tyre squeals there, but who was he to judge? He'd done a fair bit of burning rubber in his day.

And there she was, all alone, stacking the chairs. She pulled them towards the right, to a door, disappearing into her office, and he grabbed his chance, legging it across the car park and inside, where he locked the Yale then switched off the lights. Turned on the lamp attached to his forehead, the black band bringing on the urge to scratch where his scalp had got sweaty. He

3

positioned himself. Waited again. She'd probably be collecting her bag, putting on her jacket.

The sound of the handle being pushed down churned his stomach. This was it. He was doing this.

Bloody hell...

He stood in front of the office door, which opened, his beam illuminating her face, a frown wiggling her brow, then her mouth gaped open, a pathetic squeal shooting out.

"What...? Who...?"

A little whimper came from her then, and he shoved her bony chest, her blinking in fright or because of the torch, he didn't much give a shit. She staggered backwards, her handbag slipping off her shoulder and hitting the wiry-carpeted floor.

"Switch that computer on," he said, using The Voice of Fear, the one he'd been practising. Christ, he wanted to laugh. This was *insane*. "Go on, do what I said."

She scrabbled to the desk, snivelling. Her bottom lip quivered. Blimey, such a sight she made, what with the tears that'd sprung out, dribbling down her cheeks.

"What...what do you want from me?" She stood behind the desk, hands flat on it, her wedding and engagement rings loose where she'd lost weight from having stomach flu—she'd been telling everyone about it. "Why are you here?"

"You ask too many questions. *I said* switch the fucking thing on." He moved to stand beside her so she could see what she was doing via the torchlight.

Hands shaking, she managed to boot the thing up, using a password.

"Now find my name and cancel my fines." He'd only been a day late bringing the books back—hadn't finished reading, had he—and she'd slapped him with a big fat penalty, more than usual, because: *'You're always doing this and you need to learn a lesson.'*

Well, who was learning a lesson now, eh?

A giggle popped out. *Shit.*

"This isn't funny," she said. "You're scaring me."

"That's the idea, you dopey bint. Now do what I said."

"I can't if I don't know your name."

This was the part where he'd have to go through with it if he told her who he was. No going back. If he did this, did her in, he'd have to do all of them. Was he ready?

He couldn't let her live, knowing who he was. But that was the idea, wasn't it? Still, he had a moment of indecision, where he could still walk away and forget the plan.

Fuck it. "Zac Ferguson."

"You?" She whipped her head round and stared at him. "You little..."

"Not so little anymore, as you well know."

"You always were a—"

He wanted to slap her. "Shut your mouth. Take off my fine. Now."

She frowned. "Why are you talking like that? Your voice is all—"

"Why are you ignoring me? I'm telling you, if you don't do what I said..." He gritted his teeth. Should have known she'd be difficult. She was a stubborn piece. Trust him to pick *her* as the first one. Maybe it'd get easier after this.

She blinked rapidly. "You wait until the police hear about this."

"Look..." He sighed. Took the gun out of his waistband. She didn't need to know it wasn't real. He held it up in his gloved hand, pointing the business end at her. "See this? I'll blow your fucking head off in a minute if you're not careful." A rush of endorphins flounced through him.

"Zac..."

"Don't you 'Zac' me." He pressed the muzzle to her temple, hard. "Do what I said!" He was getting arsey now—well, more than he had been at any rate—and it lent him courage. Had him feeling all powerful and shit.

"Oh God, you're serious..."

"What did you think, I was having a fucking laugh? Get on with it."

She clicked the mouse and accessed the file she needed. "This isn't necessary." The cursor jiggled with her fright. "You really ought to—"

"*You* ought to shut up. One more word, and you're toast." He'd always wanted to say that.

She got into his file and removed his fine, the princely sum of twenty quid. What a joke. She'd probably plucked that amount out of the air to get back at him for that cough. When he'd received the letter telling him how much it was, that had been it. The final straw. It was her fault he was doing this—to all of them. If she'd just left him alone, none of this would be happening. He'd controlled his emotions just fine until she'd set him off. Then he'd thought about everyone who'd upset him, and here they were.

He sniffed. "Now take a load of other ones off random people."

She did.

"Close the computer down." He gave the gun a stiff nudge, and her head jerked to the side from the force. "That's it. Good. Pick up your bag."

She did that, and he pressed the gun into her back as they left the room and walked through the library. Front door open, she fumbled in her pocket.

"What are you doing?" he snapped.

"Getting the keys out! I need them to lock up from the outside." She spun to face him, her skin pasty, or it might just be from his torch.

"Leave it open. You won't be around tomorrow to unlock it. I don't want your assistant coming here and not being able to use the loo to chuck up."

She set the Yale so it was on the latch. "What are you *talking* about?" More tears, her lip wobbling again.

God, he wanted to bash her face in with the gun. Whack and whack so she didn't look like herself anymore. "She'll be sick when she finds you."

"Please, Zac, don't do this…"
"I'll do what I bloody well like."
And he did.

CHAPTER ONE

Michele Oberlander cupped the large spider and set it free in the back garden. There had been a few of the bigger buggers lately, the sort with plump bodies and long hairy legs. They didn't bother her, but they *did* bother her daughter. The last thing she needed was a call at work asking her to nip home and take the spider away.

She locked up and grabbed her bag, then jumped in the car. Well, jumped was a bit of a stretch, but she was in a good mood, so she hadn't slouched inside like she had the past few weeks. This was the last day before she had a month off, and she couldn't bloody wait for the break. The cruise she'd booked was due to set sail on Saturday, and she was eager to visit different places along the route—France, Portugal, Italy. Talk about excited. It had taken years to save for it. Lots of hard work, extra hours.

She drove to the library, ready to face the bookish people who loved the written word as much as she did. Then there was Susan Burrow, her boss, who'd been helpful in finding the tourism books they'd browsed during the quiet times. Between them, they'd worked out the best restaurants at every port and which markets to visit for leather goods and souvenirs. Michele's notebook was stuffed to the gills with information.

She turned into the car park and came to a quick stop halfway across. Susan's red Mini was in front of the library, like always, but Susan herself... What was she doing on the ground? Goosebumps sprouting all over her, Michele shot out of her car and ran towards Susan.

God, what the hell had happened? Had she fallen?

Nearer now, Michele slowed. Something wasn't right. Susan's blouse... The buttons were undone, and the fronts were bunched beside her arms. And gold circles, small, dotted her stomach. Blood, there was blood around her navel and something sticking out of it. Michele took one step closer, her heart hammering. Susan's black shoe, it was on its side next to her foot with more blood on it. Was that a *toe* in her belly button? And her face...

Michele couldn't stand to look anymore. Sickened and scared out of her mind, she ran back to her car and got in, engaged the central locking, then reached across to the passenger seat and fumbled in her bag for her phone. The bloody thing...she couldn't get a grip on it, her palms sweating, her fingers useless. She felt ill and swallowed, her breathing coming out ragged.

"Shit. *Shit!*"

Finally, she pulled her mobile free of whatever it had caught against and swiped the screen. Dialled nine-nine-nine. Told them, "My friend. My boss. I think she's dead..."

CHAPTER TWO

Already hot at nine in the morning, the summer day promised to be a belter. Heat shimmers rose off the asphalt in the library car park, and Bethany swiped her forehead. Sweat had beaded as soon as she'd got out of her car. Why had she thought wearing a long-sleeved top was a good idea? Mike, her partner, stood beside her, him in short sleeves, and they both glanced around for a woman called Michele Oberlander.

With Fran and Leona back in the incident room looking into the deceased, Susan Burrow, it was up to Bethany and Mike to get answers out here.

"Ah, that must be her," she said, nudging Mike then making her way to a white Kia, a woman sitting inside it, the driver's-side window open.

"Hello. Michele, isn't it?" She bent over to peer inside. "I'm DI Bethany Smith, and this is DS Mike Wilkins. Do you feel up to talking?" Bethany didn't tell the woman she had no choice. You find a body, you'd better be prepared for a barrage of questions and to repeat yourself several times.

"Oh, yes…" Michele got out and closed the door. Her face held the expression of someone who'd had the fright of their life, and that was probably too close to the truth for the poor love.

Bethany indicated they should go to the edge of the parking area for privacy. "There's shade over there as well. It's a bit too warm, isn't it?" Talking about normal things tended to calm some people. "Are you a summer lover?"

Michele nodded, her eyes red, cheeks damp from tears.

"One hell of a shock for you." Mike walked beside them.

"It was. I just can't get over it." Michele shuddered. "She was… Oh God, the state of her."

Bethany had sympathy. Although it was her job, she didn't like looking at dead bodies either. Mind

14

you, who did? Unless you counted weirdos or Presley Zouche, the ME. He earned his bread and butter from it. She couldn't imagine choosing that profession, but each to their own.

They came to a stop in front of a long row of hedges that bordered the rear of the car park, a couple of trees beyond that, their branches stretching over to create a leafy parasol, and the relief from not being baked to death was instant.

Michele clutched her phone to her chest, her whole body shaking, and Bethany felt for her, but they had a killer to catch, and sympathy could only go so far.

"Sorry to do this to you, but we'll need you to go through it again," Bethany said. "I realise you've spoken to an officer already."

"Yes, I did."

"Talitia Hill? Lovely girl, isn't she."

Michele nodded again. "The man was nice, too. I felt so much better once they'd arrived. After...after I'd seen Susan, I got scared that someone was hanging around, watching me. I convinced myself they were in the bushes down there." She pointed to the far corner.

Bethany thought about where that led. Behind those bushes and the cluster of trees was a residential street. Someone along there might have seen something, so it was a good job she'd already asked Tory Yates and Nicola Eccles to do house-to-house as soon as Rob Quarry on the front desk had rung Bethany to let her know about this mess.

"I imagine that must have been unsettling. So, tell us what happened." Bethany smiled to put her at ease.

Michele's story was like most others told by people who'd discovered a body. Their shock. Their horror. Their inability to process what they'd seen. Then the reality kicked in—*This is a dead person!*—and the need to call for help grabbed them.

Michele had come to a particularly gruesome part of the telling. The imagery of a toe sitting in someone's belly button...not something Bethany enjoyed first thing in the morning, and Michele's description was vivid enough to create a grisly picture.

"And she's your boss, you say." Bethany cocked her head.

Mike had his pen poised over his notebook.

"Yes. She's worked here for years." Michele slid her phone into her jeans pocket then wiped her palms down her thighs. Nervous sweat? Fear? "Her husband..."

"It's all right, we'll be going to see him. A family liaison officer is with him at the moment, so don't worry." Bethany smiled again. "Do you know of anyone who would want to do this to Susan?"

"No!" An immediate answer, definite. "She's so nice. I can't think of anybody she might have upset to this degree."

"You said: *to this degree*. Has she upset someone to a lesser one?"

16

"Of course. We both have. Our jobs aren't as quiet as you might think. People get upset if a book isn't in, or if we fine them, or if they get here just as we're closing and we don't let them in. We're shouted at, get called all sorts."

Who would have thought it? Bethany's previous idea of booklovers being gentle had just been slaughtered. Maybe people liked reading so much they were prepared to get arsey about certain things. "Surely not everyone is like that," she said.

"No, just a few. Most are wonderful."

That was something then. Readers rampaging through Shadwell if they couldn't check books out today, what with the library having to be kept closed, didn't appear to be anything she needed to worry about. No murder by hardback in her future.

"Do you recall their names, the people who aren't pleasant?" she asked.

Michele shook her head. "No. We just deal with them and move on."

Bumholes. "Okay. Did you touch Susan at all?"

Michele hugged herself. "God, no. I ran to my car. I should have checked if she had a pulse, shouldn't I, not just left her there, but she was…I knew she was dead. Her skin was pale, and she… Her *face*…"

Having not seen the victim yet, Bethany had no idea what Michele referred to. A glance over at the front of the library didn't show anything except a huge tent that hid Susan's car and her body. A SOCO van had been parked as far away from that building as possible, near the car park entrance, as had the patrol car, and Bethany had left hers over there, too. Michele's hogged the centre, where she'd stopped in her panic to go to Susan.

There wasn't anything else to discuss with Michele, so Bethany told her she could go home.

"But what about the library?"

"What about it?" Bethany asked.

"I'm off for a month on holiday, and without Susan, there's only Vera…"

"Then the council will just have to get someone else in to help run it, won't they. It'll have to be closed for a couple of days anyway while we do a thorough search of the premises—we don't yet know if anyone was inside with her yesterday after everyone had gone home. Where will you be going?" While Bethany didn't suspect Michele, she'd still need to know her whereabouts for the immediate future.

"A cruise. I go Saturday. Come back next month."

"Okay, give Mike those details."

She did, then said, "Susan would have been here late last night for the book club."

Bethany's interest was piqued. "Oh, really? What time does that finish?"

"Ten."

"And would there be a list inside of who attended?"

"No, it's a drop-in effort."

Bollocks. "What time does the club start?"

"Seven."

Three hours talking about books? "Okay, thanks. Sorry, but we have to get on. Enjoy your time away."

Bethany left Mike chatting to her and strode to Talitia, who stood at the entrance to the car park, intercepting traffic inclined to drive in, plus those on foot wanting to go into the library.

"Having fun, are we?" Bethany asked.

"Um...no. D'you know what, some people are just rude." Talitia huffed. "There's no need for it. They act like it's my fault this is happening."

"The joys of dealing with the public. What sort of shit are they coming out with?"

"Oh, they'll get a fine if the book isn't handed in today. The copy they reserved of *Balloons and Gondoliers* or whatever the hell it's called is arriving this morning. They need *The Starling Flies* for English Lit. They *need* to use the internet to send off a job application. As I've explained, nicely, death doesn't care about books or going online, or how it affects other people."

"The killer doesn't either."

"Hmm, but I couldn't really say that, and of course, I can't be rude to them. It's just some days..." Talitia sighed. "Trying not to let the cat out of the bag is difficult at times, even though the tent gives it away."

"I know, but we don't want mass panic. That's never good." She glanced down the road at some gimp parking on the verge and getting out of his vehicle. "Oh, bloody Nora..."

19

"What...?" Talitia turned that way. "Oh. Just what I don't need."

"I'll deal with him, don't you worry." Bethany stomped towards Peter Uxbridge, the crime reporter for *The Shadwell Herald*. "Get back in your car, you. Nothing to poke your nose into here."

"A phone call tells me different." He smirked.

God, she detested him. If she could get away with punching that smug look off his face, she would. Unfortunately, she couldn't, so she settled with, "Go or be cautioned for remaining at a crime scene after being asked to leave. I'm being nice— at the moment."

He assessed their surroundings, raising his eyebrows as though she'd just spoken a load of old tosh. "I don't see any police tape."

"People don't like smartarses." *Translation: I don't like you.*

"I couldn't give a nun's chuff *what* people like." He shoved his hands in his trouser pockets and rocked back and forth. "I'm just doing my job."

"And I'm just doing mine, so we're on the same wavelength on that. Who told you about this?" *Is it his 'contact at the police force who shall remain anonymous'?* Whoever that was bordered on wrecking cases at times, the loose-lipped prat.

"I had a call from a reader, if you must know. She came to switch her books out but was told she couldn't."

"So you just so happened to ask if there was a tent erected, I bet." Her nerves jangled.

"None of your business."

"It is my bloody business."

"And it's mine." He bristled. "It's part of my work."

"Well, sod off and earn your wage writing about something else. If you don't..."

"You haven't got enough bollocks to arrest me." His lips curled into another smirk, and he sniffed as though she didn't smell nice.

Could she be bothered to argue with him? No. "Look, go away."

He laughed. "See? Told you. All mouth and no trousers, you are." He got in his car, backed up a few metres, and parked there.

Bethany let out a jerky breath and returned to Talitia. "Okay, much as he's a dickhead, he shouldn't give you any gyp. So long as he stays where he is, that's fine." She couldn't be doing with arresting him, not with all the hassle he'd cause afterwards. He'd write a disparaging piece for the paper, putting the police down, and Chief Kribbs would twitter in her earhole about it. "Right, I have a body to look at."

"Sucks to be you," Talitia said, giving a sympathy frown.

"And you." Bethany nodded at a ginger woman steaming their way. "Good luck with that."

She laughed and walked off, meeting up with Mike, who patted the roof of Michele's car, then the woman reversed out of the car park. Talitia stopped her and held out the log to sign, then the poor bugger was off. Not a fantastic start to her

21

holiday, but she'd have sea and cocktails to help her get over it, which was a damn sight more than anyone else.

"Suppose we'd better get this over and done with then, matey." She slung an arm across Mike's shoulders. "And to think, when we first started on this team, we thought we'd have an easy ride."

"Naïve, the pair of us. What Michele said about that toe…" He went grey. "I thought about that case where the woman had all hers cut off, d'you remember?"

"I can remember but choose not to." Unless it woke her at night or something triggered it—like Mike bloody well mentioning it. "Right, let's get togged up, then we'll go in."

Glen Underby stood beside the tent flap next to a cardboard box containing the usual protective clothing. While Mike chatted to the PC, Bethany fished around, taking out what they needed. She handed Mike's over then got dressed, nerves biting her guts at what she'd see when she went in the tent.

"Right, let's do this." She waved at Glen, then dipped inside.

"Good morning to you," Isabelle Abbott, the lead SOCO said. "And what a bloody rotten one it is when presented with a mess like this."

Bethany kept her sights off the body and, with Mike to her left, she stepped closer. "Not a good morning at all, but never mind."

Other SOCOs worked on Susan's car to the right.

"This one's a puzzle," Isabelle said. "The killer's saying something. Glad I'm not you, because I can't work it out. Maybe I'm having a thick day, who knows."

Bethany's attention snagged on chalk lines to the left of the body, something Michele had failed to mention. Maybe the actual corpse had captured her concentration and she hadn't thought to look farther afield. Someone had drawn the grid of noughts and crosses, and one cross sat in the top-left corner.

"A kid's game?" Mike shook his head. "I don't even want to begin to imagine what's going on in the killer's mind."

"I'm afraid we're going to have to," Bethany said.

"And as for the state of Susan..." He retched behind his face mask.

"That bad, is it?" Bethany asked.

"She's got an upside-down, wrong-way-round seven on her forehead."

Ah. Michele mentioned the face. "Okay..." She shivered at the image that conjured.

"It's been carved there." He coughed.

Carved? Dear God.

"Like I said, the killer's saying something." Isabelle moved near the victim's feet—not too close; blood was on the ground. "Come on, Beth. Have a gander, will you? You two need to get your heads together on this, see what you come up with."

Bethany sighed and shifted her focus to Susan. And wished she hadn't. Someone had a sick and twisted mind to have come up with this. Her blouse fronts had been pushed to the sides to reveal her torso, her white bra, tiny blobs of blood spatter marring the lace. As well as having a bloodied toe sticking out of her navel, small gold discs had been placed on her belly above it. They appeared glued, lying flat to the skin.

"Have you tried moving one of those?" she asked.

"Not yet," Isabelle said. "We've only just finished taking photos, and I heard you talking out there so wanted to wait for you to come and watch."

"You're wicked to me," Bethany said, a smile creeping in.

"It passes the time, gives me a giggle knowing you can't stand this sort of thing. Want me to do it now?"

"Let me just look at the rest of her first."

Strangulation marks marred her neck. Blood drips had dribbled down from the carving on her forehead, over her eyes, her temples, into her ears, suggesting she'd been alive—or only just dead—when the killer had created it, otherwise, fifteen minutes or so after her heart had stopped, the blood would have begun the coagulation process, thickening, clotting. She winced at the pain Susan must have experienced—the carving was about a centimetre wide, and it was obvious the shape had been cut first, then the skin lifted out, the depth of the wound a few millimetres.

"Why draw a seven upside down?" she mused. "Looks more like a tick to me."

"Blimey, I can see it now you've mentioned it," Mike said.

Bethany forced herself to venture lower. One black shoe was still on, but the other, for her right foot, rested on its side on the tarmac. The toe beside the big one had been snipped off, a clean cut, and she shut her imagination down before she entertained what had been used to do it.

"Right, let's see if those discs are glued on," she said.

Isabelle crouched next to Susan and reached out with tweezers. She lifted the edge, and the disc rose. "Um, okay…" She peered closer. "These are bloody drawing pins. Tacks."

Bethany's skin went cold. She stared at the clues left behind in order from the top.

Tick.

Tack.

Toe.

Then she stared at the noughts and crosses chalked out. "The American version of the game." She pointed to the drawing. "Tic-tac-toe."

"Fucking hell…" Mike breathed. "What sort of nutter are we dealing with here?"

"More to the point," Bethany said, "what have they done with the skin from that tick?"

CHAPTER THREE

Zac lounged in front of the telly, staring at Eamonn Holmes gassing on about climate change. Zac reckoned it existed, but some knob on the phone-in didn't agree and argued the toss with Holmes. Of course it was real. The weather didn't just decide to go all weird by itself, did it?

In the kitchen, his missus, Jambrea, waffled on, but Zac tuned her out. She'd been going off on one for ages now, saying she'd woken up last night and he hadn't been home. He hadn't, but that was beside the point. Seemed the bottle of wine he'd plied her with hadn't kept her asleep; she woken up for a wee. She wouldn't listen to him when he'd said she must be mistaken, that he'd kipped on the sofa in the conservatory—even though she'd admitted to not checking there so couldn't prove otherwise.

Stupid cow.

She was getting right on his nerves, whining, her voice filtering through. Wanker this, twat that, waste of space, loser. Whatever. He'd heard them all before, but he wouldn't have to listen to it for much longer. He'd saved the bottom-right corner of the noughts and crosses grid just for her. She'd be the last one, the finale, but if she didn't watch herself, she'd be next. There was only so much a man could take.

"Are you shagging about?" Jambrea called. "Is that what you're doing? Because if it is, you can just fuck right off out of here."

That'd be a bit difficult, seeing as it was his house. If anyone was fucking right off, it was her. She could go back to her mum's for the few days before he killed her. At least he'd get some peace then, to think.

"Well?" she said, something or other clattering. She was probably unloading the dishwasher and shoving the pans away in a huff. "Where were you?"

He jabbed the OFF button on the remote, the TV going as blank as his loving feelings for her. She'd nagged that love out of him, and he'd just been going through the motions for the past two years. Shame, because the first three had been great. Did everyone go through that? Did all relationships have blips where you wondered what the hell you'd seen in them?

"In the bloody conservatory," he shouted. "How many times do I have to tell you?"

"As many as it takes for me to believe you."

"That'll be for the next week then," he mumbled. Christ, couldn't she leave a tired man alone? Fair enough, she didn't know he was tired, that he'd been out all evening, plus into the early hours, waiting, hoping a car would come along and the driver discovered Susan bloody Burrow. That would have made his day. Instead, he'd come home, had a kip, then got up at the arse crack of dawn and waited behind the hedges again until that muppet, Michele, had turned up. Fuck me, that had been funny, seeing her face, how scared she was.

"What are *you* smiling at?" Jambrea snapped.

Fuck. She stood in the living room doorway, hands on hips, glaring at him. Her in this kind of mood wasn't good.

"I wasn't smiling." *Was I?*

"Do you have to lie about every little thing? I just *saw you doing it!*" She eyed him as though she wanted to kill him.

She's got no idea it's the other way around.

He'd better watch himself. Getting lost inside his head while she was about wasn't good. "I wasn't aware I'd done it." At least he hadn't lied about *that.*

"Bullshit." She paused. "When are you going to get ready? I need to go to Sainsbury's."

Why couldn't she go to Lidl or Aldi like everyone else around here? What was it about her insisting that neighbours seeing the Sainsbury's name on their carrier bags was important now he ran his own business? Like they'd gone up in the world. But they were the same people underneath. Maybe they ought to use the Sainsbury's bags to put their Aldi shopping in. People in their street would still think they were richer now.

Thinking of his business reminded him he hadn't picked up the latest takings from Erica Orloff yet, so he was a bit strapped for cash. Jambrea was spending it like water.

Times past, she'd accused him of sleeping with Erica, but come on, Erica was his money collector for the small loan company he'd recently set up, sharp as fuck, hard as nails, and she wouldn't look twice at him in that way. Not when she was seeing that beefcake of hers, who'd break Zac's neck inside a second if he thought any funny business was going on. And she was Russian. They were scary. Erica was a bit of all right, he'd admit that, but dipping his wick in her particular candle wasn't a wise move. He thought about it, though. A lot.

"If you want to go to Sainsbury's, we need to see Erica first." He pushed off the sofa. "She's got the collection dosh."

"Yeah, and she takes twenty percent off that before she hands it over. Bloody extortion." Jambrea backed into the hallway and scooped up her high heels, some Jimmy whatevers she'd begged him for the other week. He could've bought a secondhand car for the price they'd set him back.

"Nope, that's her cut, her wages." He jammed a hand through his hair so he didn't jam it in Jambrea's mush. "She does all the dirty work, you know that. She takes a risk every time she knocks on someone's door."

"Not when she has her bloke with her she doesn't. That Lenny would beat the shit out of them if they didn't pay up."

So would Erica. Rumour had it she was a killer for hire. He couldn't imagine it himself, but he didn't fancy pushing her to see how far he could go before she snapped. Even if she *wasn't* a killer, she was ballsy enough to do the job he needed her for, and that was all that mattered. "Well, then, that twenty percent is for the pair of them, so shut your trap."

He brushed past her, into the hallway, sad their relationship had come to this. They'd been solid once, always laughing, and Jambrea had been a right goer. Then he'd lost his job, and it had all gone to shit. She'd kept them afloat on top of his Jobseeker's until he'd nicked seventeen grand from beneath the bed of some old dear he'd cut the grass for. Then he'd had the idea to be a loan shark. Stupid of him not to have kept some cash back for them to live off, but that was him all over. Mr Impetuous. Until he'd thought of killing Susan Burrow, and his big plan had hatched. Then he'd become careful. Vigilant. If he applied it to his working day, he'd go far.

It was convenient the old lady had died of a heart attack—the shock of having her money stolen. No one had even known it was there. She'd carked it before she could tell anyone the 'gardener' had swiped it from under her beaky nose.

He stared at the Jimmy's on his girlfriend's feet. He'd sell the fuckers if she didn't stop badgering him. That'd teach her.

"Come on then!" She slung her bag strap on her shoulder.

So he didn't bite back at her, he grabbed the car keys and left the house, Jambrea tottering behind him down the path, her heels clip-clopping, and if he didn't rein in his temper, he'd start a proper row, and *that* would give the neighbours something to talk about other than orange carrier bags.

In his old Golf, he revved the engine while she got her seat belt on, then drove off to the other side of the estate, the posher half. Erica lived in a well nice house—dodgy money, and lots of it, did that for you—and he parked outside, cringing, like he always did, at the state of his car giving away the fact he wasn't as rich as he made out.

He stayed put. That was the deal. While people might see them talking at his car, going into her house was a no-no.

The venetian blinds parted like a massive, blank eye, and a shiver went through him. Lenny, it had to be, nosing out to see if any trouble was coming to their door. With their line of work, it wouldn't be surprising.

The shiny black front door opened, and the woman herself came out, all poise and grace, at odds with the killer rumour. Her white-blonde hair hung in a blunt cut to her shoulders. To look at her, you'd never know she could knock your fucking block off with one hand-chop or a karate kick. She tended not to if she could help it, said she risked breaking a nail, but people knew all about her and what she was capable of. Skin-tight, black leather shorts and a white, lowcut T-shirt both moulded to her body, showing off the goods he couldn't buy let alone touch. She carried a fat padded brown envelope, the size of A4 paper.

"Eyes in your head," Jambrea sniped and flipped the visor down to check herself in the mirror on the back.

"For fuck's sake! I'm not doing anything wrong and you accuse me." He smacked the steering wheel, frustrated, and the horn blared. "Now look what you've made me do."

"Don't you try that gaslighting shit on me. I've read all about that on Facebook. I didn't *make* you do anything. *You* slammed the wheel. Take responsibility for your own actions." She took lippy out of her bag and applied it.

"Shut up. Erica's here." He wound the window down and smiled. "Morning." He'd almost added 'love' but nipped that in the bud pretty sharpish, what with earholes sitting next to him. She'd go mad at that.

Erica bent over and leant her tanned forearms on the door, tits peering over the scooped neckline, two massive dough balls from Pizza Express. "Trouble with Customer Three," she said quietly. "Lenny nearly had to break nose."

Her Russian accent did funny things to Zac down below. "Oh. What was the problem?"

"He was ten pounds short."

What? Just a tenner? What was her problem? "Well—"

"You do not allow any lapses," she said. "If you do, they run rings around you. They take piss. You look like a laughing stock."

"So what happened?"

"He asked neighbour. Neighbour gave ten pounds."

God, if she kept talking like that, he was likely to embarrass himself, and with Jambrea beside him, that wasn't a good idea. "But that's why I employ you, to deal with that side of things."

"It is, but I am just giving you warning. If he tries to mug me off again, Lenny will break nose

34

and maybe knock out teeth. The customer borrowed a lot—how will he pay back the next thousand? I worry about these things."

Customer Three had borrowed eight of the granny's stolen cash, set to pay back double, a grand payment every fortnight. Erica kept track in her little notebook—"Never put it on computer," she'd said—and Lenny had a copy of it. Zac couldn't be arsed keeping a third, and anyway, who was he to argue with these two if some cash went astray? So long as he got a wedge, he was happy. He liked his nose and teeth where they were, thanks. They didn't need rearranging.

Taking the envelope from her, he said, "Cheers. Everyone else cough up all right?" Several customers paid smaller amounts, but they still had to repay double. He stuffed the envelope under his seat.

"They did. See you next week."

"I'll let you know in the meantime if anyone new borrows." He gave her dough balls one last, longing look, then pressed the button to raise the window.

She took her arms away, sauntered around the front of the car, and walked into her place. The venetian blinds snapped back into straight lines.

So Lenny had watched the whole exchange.

"I want her boobs," Jambrea said.

So do I. "Too expensive." He drove off.

"You've probably got enough in that envelope."

"Probably, but you want to go to Sainsbury's, then there's the rent, the electric, the fucking council tax—I want to pay them six months in advance to give us some breathing space. Like we should have done when I nicked the old dear's cash."

"You owe me for paying the bills when you had no job."

"The Jimmy's paid you back."

"Tight bastard."

Annoying bitch.

He continued driving, ignoring her chirping at him, wishing he could have buried his face in Erica's cleavage and forgotten everything for a while. He took a different route at the last minute, doing ten miles per hour along the road by the library. A copper stood at the car park entrance, and a large van, police car, and a third vehicle huddled close to the edge. A fourth car sat on the verge.

The policewoman flagged him down, and he just about shit his boxers, then gave himself a reminder that he'd done this one on foot, so his car hadn't been recognised. He stopped and yet again lowered the window.

The PC bent over—no chance of seeing her tits. Sadness.

"Hello, sir. We're questioning everyone who goes past. Were you around here last night or the early hours of the morning?"

He shook his head. "Nope, I was at home with the missus." He jerked a thumb at Jambrea and stared across at the tent. "What's going on there then?"

"A crime has been committed, sir."

"Blimey."

"What sort of crime?" Jambrea piped up. "Tents can only mean one thing. I watch all the shows so know these things."

Shut up, will you? "It's not our business," he told her, then smiled at the copper as if to say: *What can you do, eh?* "As I said, we were at home."

"Okay, sir, thank you." The PC waved him on, glanced behind his car, and raised her hand at another motorist.

Zac drove off, legs like jelly, his foot dancing on the accelerator so the car shot forward. When he'd spoken to Susan in the library last night then killed her, he'd become a different person, full of power and confidence. Now, he was a regular bloke, worried he'd get caught and have to go to prison. He wanted anger to visit him so he'd feel better again. To get the ball rolling, he lashed out, giving Jambrea a backhander to the face.

"Fucking hell, Zac! What was that for?" She held her cheek, eyes watering.

Breathing. "Accusing me of looking at Erica's tits."

"But you were."

"They were *there*, hanging out, but I didn't purposely look. Christ, you make me out to be a pervert or something."

"Don't you ever hit me again," she said, voice low.

"Or what?"

"Or I'll ring the police and tell them you weren't home last night."

Shit, does she know? Have I been acting weird lately and she's sussed me out? "Piss off." He turned into the Sainsbury's car park, grabbed a bay as close to the shop as he could, and cut the engine. He took a few notes from the envelope and put them in his wallet, tucked the envelope under his arm, got out, and stormed to the trolleys, shoving a quid in one to release the chain. As he strode through the automatic doorway, Jambrea appeared at his side.

"The tits, Zac," she said. "I want the tits."

Fuck it. He'd have to make out he was giving in just to shut her up, stop her going on and on about them—on and on about him not being home last night. The thing was, would it just stop at a decent rack, or would she keep asking for stuff between now and when he killed her? So long as the money was there, she'd be after it.

He'd put a stop to it, before it got started. "No. Yours are fine as they are."

"Then you'll just have to wait and see what I do, won't you."

Where had this snide part of her come from?

"If you try to get me in the shit, for whatever it is you think I've done, and I get put away, do you think Erica and Lenny are going to hand the money over to you instead?"

"Of course they will."

"Dream on, love. I've already made provisions." He moved over to the veg and threw a cloud of broccoli in the trolley. It bounced then came to rest, the stem wedging into the bottom.

"What do you mean?" She snatched up a bag of spuds and tossed them beside the broccoli. "Sod it. Forgot I'm not eating carbs." She returned the potatoes, looking at them longingly.

Probably thinking about all that mash she likes. "You've accused me of shagging about, fancying Erica, and God knows what else this morning." He selected a packet of wonky carrots, just for something to do. "Do you blame me for making sure my money's safe if you grass me up?"

"You took it from an old lady, Zac."

He laughed, incredulous. "Didn't bother you when it bought those shoes on your trotters, though, did it?"

She blushed.

As well she might. "Keep your gob shut and your nose out of my business." He put the carrots back and picked up a fresh ginger root shaped like a gun. Held it. Pointed it at her. "Or you might find yourself in more crap than you ever imagined."

Her eyes widened, and she backed away, almost going arse over tit her heels were so high. "You wouldn't."

Oh, I would. I will. "Try me."

CHAPTER FOUR

Presley entered the tent, scattering Bethany's thoughts from the 'game' idea they'd been mulling over. If the noughts and crosses grid hadn't been chalked out, she wouldn't have made the connection. What did it mean? What significance did it have? Or was it one of those obscure reasons only the killer knew about? She was used to that, and sometimes, she ended an investigation not knowing the 'why' at all and had to be content with the fact the criminal had been caught.

"Morning," Presley said, coming to stand beside Mike. He looked sad. Tired. Like he didn't want to be here today. "Oh. That's a bit unpleasant." He frowned. "The carving and the toe."

"And the drawing pins in her belly aren't?" Isabelle asked, always one to rile him if she could get away with it. She got some form of perverse pleasure in winding him up, and they bickered every time they were near each other.

"Of course they are," Presley said, "but the other two stood out first, which is why I mentioned them. Please don't start on me today, there's a dear. Despite me not wanting to give you the satisfaction of knowing you've annoyed me, I'm likely to bite your head off." His clipped tone said he wasn't in the mood for her shit.

Would she back off? *I doubt it.* Saying 'don't' was a red rag to a bull. Isabelle was *more* likely to peck at him now—harder.

"I mean it," he said and gave her a damning glare. "I found my cat dead this morning."

Oh. Fuck.

"So sorry," Bethany said, unsure what to do with herself now. He wasn't the type to appreciate a pat on the arm or whatever, nor did he like any fuss.

42

Presley gave her a thankful smile. "He was old. It was expected but..." He appeared to shrug off what he'd been about to say, as if he couldn't allow anyone in, to know he hurt the same as everybody else. "Now...what on earth is going on here?" He placed his bag down and removed his clipboard. "I want to sketch this for studying later. Those tacks appear random, but there may well be a pattern I just can't see yet."

Isabelle glanced at Bethany, guilt written all over her. Bethany shook her head to tell her not to mention the cat—he'd changed the subject, closing it, and clearly didn't want a discussion in that regard.

"Yes, we'll study the photos as well," Isabelle said. "Between us, we may come up with something."

Once he'd finished drawing, everyone else standing there in silence, awkward, he got busy with the ear temperature. Mike wandered off towards a SOCO who dusted Susan's car for prints on the other side. Bethany didn't blame him. With Presley upset and Isabelle treading on eggshells, it didn't make for a comfortable few minutes.

"About ten-thirty last night," Presley said. "Or thereabouts. There's a piece of thread caught between two of her front teeth. So cotton material, perhaps. Black."

Bethany leant forward to have a look. Susan's teeth were bared in a death smile, or a grimace, whichever way you wanted to view it. So she'd either had something stuffed in her mouth or a gag going across, one that tied at the side or back. The edges of her lips didn't look sore from the latter, though; a gag like that tended to chafe and, depending on how tight it was, it bruised.

Presley tried to lift her arm. "Rigor, almost in full, so that ties in with my estimate—eight to twelve hours after death, complete rigidity."

"Yes, she worked late last night."

"I'd say strangulation was the cause."

Bethany had a thought. "Mike?" she called.

He popped his head round the Mini. "Yep?"

"Let's nip inside the library, see what we get there. Izz, are you coming?"

Isabelle nodded. "I've already had a look, didn't notice anything much, but you could do with a walk round. There aren't any cameras whatsoever, inside or out, so that's a bummer."

"Okay, well, I need to get a feel for what might have happened in there, although... Hang on, how did you get in?"

"It was left open," Isabelle said. "So maybe she didn't even get a chance to lock up. The door is on the latch. Maybe someone waited out here, approached her before she'd managed to get the keys out—you'll see there's a Yale plus a mortise."

They left the tent, and Isabelle went inside the building first, followed by Mike then Bethany. It appeared as you'd expect any library, neat and tidy, the smell of books highly prevalent, of pages turned a million times. Nothing appeared to have been moved in a scuffle, and she looked at the door. Fingerprint powder had been brushed over the lock.

Bet her prints are they last layer on it.

They walked down each of the aisles, the spines on the shelves covered in plastic jackets. Love stories, sci-fi, thrillers, chick-lit. Then they went into the public toilets, the scent of urinal blocks strong in the men's, then out again and through a doorway to an office. A lipstick was on the floor, an evidence marker beside it. Had Susan dropped it on purpose? Other than that, the room was clean.

"There was a computer, but that's already been taken in," Isabelle said. "I got the password from Michele Oberlander. We'll be able to determine what time it was last used and what was done on it. That might help quite a bit."

"Handy. The results probably won't be in for a day or so. That'll hold us up," Bethany said.

"Oh, I don't know. Digi forensics are pretty fast here, aren't they. Besides, Aradul is on shift, and you know what that means." Isabelle grinned.

"Did you have that drink with him yet?" Bethany felt sorry for the forensic bloke, who always went above and beyond to get results for Isabelle, who he fancied like mad.

"Damn, I knew I'd forgotten to do something." Isabelle laughed.

"That was yonks ago you were supposed to go out with him. I can't believe you've left him on the hook."

"Hmm. He's a nice man, so maybe I ought to ask him again, say I've been overworked, which isn't a

45

lie. Anyway, we're getting off the original subject. Aradul said he'd be on this as soon as possible."

"Okay." Bethany sighed. "I suppose we ought to go and visit Susan's husband."

She said her goodbyes and, seeing as she already had the address from Talitia earlier, she drove them to it, glad Alice Jacobs, the family liaison officer, would already have broken the news. At least that was one job Bethany and Mike didn't need to do—they hated it.

The Burrow house was modest, the middle in a terrace of five, a white SUV on the tarmac drive, which took place of a front garden. The others in the row had grass and flowerbeds, multicoloured blooms turning their faces to the sun, a couple of bees hovering, waiting to land and collect nectar. Bethany knocked, and Alice answered, stepping outside, leaving the door ajar.

"How's it going?" Bethany asked.

"He's a bit better now. Was obviously devastated when I told him." Alice smiled sadly.

"What's his name again? Me and my memory..."

"Richard. No kids living at home—their sons share a flat and are away together in Ibiza. Like the clubbing circuit apparently. He hasn't informed them yet. He's unsure whether to leave it until they get home tomorrow or phone them today. It's his choice, but I've advised he leaves it. There's nothing that can be done anyway, and it'll give him a better chance to come to terms with it himself first. Unless, of course, he needs their support, and he's said he doesn't know *what* he wants or how he's supposed to feel, so there you are."

"Let's go in then."

Alice led them to an airy kitchen, then through to a sun-trap conservatory with wicker furniture and three bookshelves crammed with novels. Richard, late forties, early fifties, sat opposite the open outer door, where an Old English Sheepdog came racing in from the garden to sit at his feet. The poor thing must be boiling with all that shaggy fur.

Bethany introduced them, and Alice announced she'd make some tea.

Bethany sat, while Mike stood, notebook at the ready.

"Mr Burrow, Richard, firstly, so sorry for your loss." She thought about the days to come, where he'd go into a spiral of grief if he didn't keep himself busy. When Bethany's husband, Vinny, had died, she'd thrown herself into work, unable to allow herself time to think too much about what she'd lost and how lonely she was without him. "We'll probably repeat questions Alice has already asked you, so if you could bear with us on that and accept my apology for it in advance..."

He nodded, staring out into the garden. Vacant, as though he'd had enough and couldn't deal with any more today, and he needed a nap. That would erase the horror of his new situation for the duration he slept, but as soon as he opened his eyes, he'd get a moment of thinking everything was how it had always been, then the knowledge would slam back in, wrecking him all over again.

And it hurts.

"Where were you last night?" she asked.

He sighed. "I had my mum and dad round for a bite to eat. Susan was at work—book club—and after dinner, me and my parents sat out here and had a few glasses of wine. It's a weekly thing, them coming over." He blinked. "It got to about twenty past ten when Susan usually would have come home, and we went back into the house, loading the dishwasher, cleaning up so she didn't walk in to a mess. By twenty to eleven, I gave Susan a ring—sometimes she stops off at a supermarket to take advantage of the twenty-four-hour shopping. Quieter, she said." He smiled wistfully, a tear plopping down his cheek.

He'll be seeing her in his head, her face, her smile...

"So, I didn't worry overly much when she didn't answer. If she was in the queue, she wouldn't have bothered. I sent a text, asking her if she'd gone to Sainsbury's or whatever, and to let me know she was okay once she'd got in the car. Mum and Dad left about five to eleven—they only live in the next street. I had a sit down in the living room, and...and the next thing I know, it's morning, and Susan hadn't come home. To top it off, I'd overslept and was going to be late for work. Then the doorbell went, and Alice stood there... God, *why* did I fall asleep? I could have gone out last night, to the library, stopped whatever... Instead, I was out of it while she was..."

He sobbed for some time, the dog getting worried and whining, resting his head on Richard's knee. Alice came in with the teas on a tray, and she handed them out, leaving Richard until last so he had a moment to compose himself. By then, Bethany and Mike had finished theirs.

If it wasn't for the fact his parents had been here at the time of Susan's death—they'd still have to verify his alibi—Bethany might have put Richard on her suspect list. However, he could have paid someone else to do it, so he wasn't completely in the clear.

"Does the game noughts and crosses mean anything to you?" She watched him carefully for his reaction.

An immediate frown, him raising his head, as though thinking, trying to recall a link. Bethany didn't hold with all that shit about staring up, how to the right meant a lie, the left meant the truth. She'd had many a liar choose the left, and she'd consciously caught herself looking right when remembering something.

"Only that I liked it as a kid," he said. "Why?"

"What about Susan? Did she enjoy playing it?"

He shrugged. "Can't say it's ever come up in all the years we've been together. She might have played it with our sons, but I just don't know... I was...I was career-focused years ago when they were small. I didn't...didn't pay enough attention."

He hiccoughed. "I left Susan to get on with it, and now I can't say sorry for it."

Bethany knew self-recrimination well—and it didn't do the mourner any good. "I'm sure Susan understood. It happens this way with many families." She was about to ask him about ticks and toes but stopped herself. He'd find out the state of his wife soon enough. "Do you know of any fallings out Susan had?"

"No, she preferred to talk things through over rowing, so any disagreements she had would have been resolved."

"No one who would be holding a grudge then?"

"No."

She hadn't expected anything else, not after speaking to Michele about her. "Okay, we'll leave you be for now." She widened her eyes to Alice, indicating they needed to talk in private. On the driveway, she said, "Did you check the sons are actually in Ibiza?"

"Yes, and uniform have been round to Richard's parents' place. They arrived and left when he said they did, although they could well have corroborated beforehand. His phone records will show whether he sent text messages or rang them to get them to say what he did, and he's given permission for his mobile supplier to send us whatever we need—I let Fran and Leona know the details will be coming their way."

"Thanks. Susan was killed about half ten, so no chance it was Richard personally," Mike said.

Alice's eyes widened. "Personally? As in, he might have paid someone else to do it? If he did, you won't find anything on his bank statements. I've had a look through them—he offered—and he said he'll send PDF equivalents when he's feeling up to it. Honestly, it isn't him."

"I agree with you," Bethany said. "We'd better go. I need to catch up with Fran and Leona and let Kribbs know what's going on. Thanks for everything."

"Not a problem, and if I find anything else out, I'll message you." Alice held up a hand then vanished inside.

On the drive back to the station, Bethany said, "There's no way what the killer did is random— that takes a lot of thought, and no one walks round with a tool to cut toes off, tacks, and a scalpel or whatever in their bag. Not to mention chalk. But was *Susan* random?"

Mike scrubbed his chin. "Serial killers...as you know, they think about it for a long time before actually doing it. Well, most of them do anyway. The thinking about it sustains them for a good while, so it wouldn't be unheard of for one of them to walk round with their kill kit, just in case. If this person has no particular victim in mind, he could have been walking home to the estate, passed the library, saw Susan about to lock up, then got the urge. I have to say, her time of death is pretty close to the end of the book club, which finished at ten. We have no way of knowing, unless we put something out on the news, who attended the book club. With no list of attendees either, one of them could have arrived with his kill kit in a bag, sat and discussed whatever book was on the agenda, left like everyone else, then waited for her outside."

Bethany could see his point, but... "We know someone stood behind those hedges at the back because of the grass being flattened—Talitia mentioned it when we first arrived on scene, if you remember, so while it *could* be random and the person waited for her there, I'm leaning more towards her knowing her killer. No signs of a struggle, no defence wounds."

"Unless she was threatened with something to keep her compliant."

"I don't know. No marks on her wrists, but she had a long-sleeved blouse on, so bindings may not have marked her. But if that tick was carved out while she was alive, wouldn't she instinctually have reached up to stop it being done? Did they sit on her hands? So much doesn't add up."

"Too many unanswered questions," Mike said.

She pulled into her spot in the station car park, and they legged it up to the incident room. Fran and Leona were busy at their desks, heads bent.

"Hi," Bethany said, going straight to one of the whiteboards. She picked up a black marker and cracked on with writing down everything from this morning. "Got anything from the searches on Susan and CCTV?"

Fran spun her chair to face the room. "She isn't on any social media personally—unusual but not unheard of—but she does run the library page so has a profile. She talks about all things library, and the post for last night's book club had six women and two men commenting to say they'd be attending. I've run their names through a search, and they're all real—no nicknames—and found their addresses. I've arranged for them all to come in at midday. I said it was to help with our enquiries. You okay with that?"

"Yep." Bethany nodded. "That's brilliant, because I was wondering how we were going to find out who they were. Leona?"

"CCTV cuts off just before the turning to the library car park. However, it's visible how many cars went there. All licence plates match to the book club members—the camera is pretty close and the images clear. I'm still going through all the other vehicles that went past both ways, and that could take some time. I've also found where Michele Oberlander arrived this morning, and it's the time she stated. Unfortunately, none of the car park is in view, so we didn't get lucky enough to capture the murder on tape. Whoever did it never used a car—or if they did, it didn't go into, or come out of, that car park."

"So someone either parked in the street behind the bushes or they came on foot." Bethany thought about that. "So we could be looking at a person who lives on that estate."

Leona nodded. "That's more than two thousand houses, by the way. Already checked. Also already checked is the estate CCTV. None except by the row of shops, as is usual, but some homes will have private cameras. It's a case of walking the estate street by street and spotting them, then asking if we can have the footage. Again, that's going to take a lot of time."

"Best get started on that sooner rather than later then," Bethany said. "You get that organised and ask the front desk to arrange for Glen Underby and Talitia Hill to come in and help you here. They'll need to be relieved beforehand, though. Talitia will be pleased. She's been getting some grief from library-goers."

"Okie dokie."

"I'm off to let Kribbs know what's going on in case I lose track of time and forget to tell him. Mike, can you get nosing into Richard Burrow and their sons, please?"

She left the room and walked down the corridor to Kribbs' office. Their conversation was short and sweet—"Get to it, Beth!"—and she returned to help her team sift through a mountain of information that might very well not throw up anything they could use.

CHAPTER FIVE

"**Y**ou need to watch your back with him," Lenny said, his rough London accent distracting Erica.

She sighed and paused from adding the recent takings to Zac's bookkeeping notepad, annoyed with herself for not doing it last night. "Who?"

"Ferguson. Zac's in too deep with this shit. In over his head. Hasn't got a clue what he's got himself into." Lenny gestured to the notepad. "You're running this show, not him. He's just the man who had the money to begin with, but people will know he's the one to go to for it, and he'll make bad decisions. Lend to liabilities. Then you're the one who has hassle if they don't pay up. And me, if you don't fancy punching someone's lights out and you get me to do it."

"But it suits me this way." She shrugged. "He is the one who will get arrested for doing illegal things. I am just an employee. I do not know anything except I have to pick up money." She nodded. "You know what I am saying?"

Lenny laughed. "Yeah, but like I said, watch him. He wouldn't think twice about blaming it on you if the shit hits the fan. There's something off about him, you mark my words."

Erica wasn't bothered. She'd got herself out of bigger scrapes before. And besides, if Zac started anything, she'd risk breaking a nail on him. One punch or slap, and he'd behave himself. "All he wants is a higher return on his money. He doesn't think about anything else. We will be able to skim some off once he is a bit more established in the game."

Zac was trying to think about something else to get his mind off what Jambrea had implied she'd do. What if she got him done for the old dear's money? He wouldn't be able to speak with The Voice of Fear and finish what he'd planned. And he was sick of switching from one emotion to another—he was okay one minute, all raring to go, and the next, he was shitting himself. He needed to maintain that anger; it'd keep him on an even keel.

He'd locked the bedroom door and now sat on the bed, his noughts and crosses blackboard on his lap. He'd bought one, about half a metre square, and had chalked on the grid. When he'd come home from killing Susan, he'd crept up here, Jambrea snoring like mad, and pulled the board out from under the bed, placing the forehead tick in the top-left box. It had stuck there, was hard now, a bit crusty on the fleshy sides, the skin rigid. Once he'd filled in all the ticks, he reckoned he'd be all right.

Footsteps.

He shoved the board under the bed.

The door handle moved down. Rattled.

"What are you doing in there?" Jambrea. "Why is the door locked? Are you playing with yourself?"

What? "No, I'm bloody not! I wanted a bit of peace, that's all."

"You've never wanted peace before. Never locked this door before either."

"There's a first time for everything," he muttered and rested back, draping an arm over his eyes. She was doing his nut in, always on his case lately. And why wasn't she at work? She usually started about twelve. "Thought you had a job to go to."

"I've got a week off, remember?"

No, he hadn't remembered. What the hell was he thinking, starting his plans now? It was no good, he'd have to go and see Erica. Well, Lenny. He'd have what he needed.

He got up, shoved his shoes on, and unlocked the door. Jambrea stood on the landing, hands on her hips again, her usual position these days. He strutted past her.

"Where are you going?" She leant over the banister rail as he went downstairs.

"Out."

"But I wanted to go for lunch."

"McDonald's is up the road. Won't take you five minutes to walk there."

"McDonald's?" she screeched. "I'm not going there!"

He shoved out of the house and into his car. What was wrong with her usual Big Mac, fries, and vanilla milkshake? Why wasn't that good enough anymore? What, did she want to go to that new swanky Italian, was that it?

Speeding off, he got round the corner, pulled over, then texted Erica, letting her know he needed to see Lenny as soon as possible. Best he didn't just turn up when they hadn't arranged it. He'd get a telling off, and he couldn't afford to lose the pair of them—they did all the grunt work so he didn't have to.

Erica: IF YOU ARE QUICK, HE WILL SEE YOU NOW.

Zac got there sharpish. The blank eye appeared in the blinds again, creepy bloody thing, then Lenny came out, tapping on the passenger-side window with a thick knuckle. Zac opened it, and Lenny poked his head inside.

"What do *you* want?" he asked, all brash.

Zac's stomach rolled over. Funny how he'd killed Susan but was scared of Lenny. "I need something to keep me asleep. I've got insomnia."

"Go to the doctor." Lenny made to stand upright.

"No, wait. I need something stronger than they'd give me."

Lenny *tsked* and stalked off, the swaggering bastard, and disappeared inside the house. He came back, one fist closed, and reached in. Dropped a bag of powder on the seat. "A thousand."

"What?" Zac stared at the bag, then at Lenny, whose head was in the car. Whatever that stuff was, it had to be good if it cost that much, not to mention highly illegal.

"Take it or leave it."

"I'll take it." It was a small price to pay in the grand scheme of things. He reached under the seat, brought the envelope out, counted the money. "How much do I need to...how much will get me a full night's kip?"

"Tip of a teaspoon." Lenny grabbed the money Zac held out, rolling it up and closing his beefy

59

hand around it. "No more than that, and not too often. Could mess with the liver and brain."

That wouldn't matter. Jambrea was going to be dead anyway, so she wouldn't need her fucking liver and brain. "Right. Okay. Cheers."

Lenny pulled his head out and stalked indoors. Zac's heart kicked up speed, an adrenaline rush, and he closed the window, then drove off, his mind going a mile a minute. If he gave Jambrea a touch more than a teaspoon tip in a glass of wine, she'd be out for the count. He could go about his business, her none the wiser. No more nosy-arsed questions.

Smiling, he nipped into the city and bought a safe from Argos, a bargain at under thirty quid. He couldn't keep the money in the car all the time, and with a pass number, it'd stop Jambrea from having sticky fingers, siphoning some off every now and then with a mind to save up for new tits. He'd had a feeling before that she'd come out and pinched some cash while he'd been in bed, the cheeky cow. And anyway, the people round here were rough. If they broke the Golf window to nick his stereo and had a root around, they'd leave richer than when they'd arrived.

While he was at it, he went to the council payment office and slapped down six months' rent and council tax. It wasn't like he could pay by bank transfer, was it. The idea of large sums of money going in gave him the jitters, and seeing as his business wasn't on the level, it was cash payments and purchases all the way.

Back home, the little bag of sleeping powder in his pocket, he ignored Jambrea calling from the kitchen, asking where he'd been, and rushed upstairs. He set the safe up with an access code—2857A—and stuffed the money inside.

"I *said*, where have you been?" she shouted again, probably from the bottom of the stairs.

God help him, but he'd slap her one in a minute. "What do you need to know for?"

"Because it's weird, that's all, you keep going out."

Why she'd said that, he had no idea. While he'd been scoping out the locations for the kills, she'd been at work, oblivious. Had her not finding him in the house last night *really* set the worm of doubt wiggling in her head? When was she going to give it the fuck up? Anger came then, and he welcomed it. He shoved the safe in his side of the wardrobe behind his boxes of trainers, a few on top so it was hidden, and joined her downstairs. She stood there clutching the newel post, and he had the mad urge to grab the back of her head and smash her face on it.

"Are you going to answer me?" she said.

"You're doing my tree in." He swept past her, into the kitchen, and flicked the kettle on.

"You're acting off," she said.

"Look, go and have a sit down in the living room. I'll make you a cuppa."

He held his breath. Waited for her to trot up behind him, have another go. He counted to thirty and turned. Fuck me, she'd done as he'd asked.

Closing the door, he took the bag out of his pocket and put a few grains on a spoon, way less than the tip, just to see what would happen and how long she'd be sparko for.

Sleepy tea made, he carried it to her, and she took it begrudgingly, giving him a filthy look. He wanted to smack the bottom of the cup so the boiling liquid went all over her, but now wasn't the time.

"Where's yours?" She blew the tea.

"Didn't want one." He switched the telly on and got the Netflix menu up. He'd put one of her shows on, that thing about housewives being real.

Thankfully, she kept her gob shut, and three quarters of the way through the brew, she was out of it. He eased the cup from her hand and left her to it, popping the cup in the dishwasher and enjoying the peace and quiet, making a mental note of the time.

Things had just become a whole lot easier.

CHAPTER SIX

Noon came soon enough, and the eight members of last night's book club had arrived and waited in the soft interview room. Wanting to get some answers, Bethany went downstairs with Mike and introduced them to the collective first, then explained they'd be spoken to one by one—but she didn't tell them why.

"We'll try to get through you all as quickly as possible, okay?"

In interview room one, Bethany and Mike on one side of the table, a Claire Billing on the other, and PC Penny Dickens beside the door, Bethany got stuck in.

"What time did you arrive at the library?"

"Five to seven," Claire said. "I waited outside with family."

"And they are?"

"Wendy and Rhiannon Tynen."

"Okay, were they there before you?"

"Yes."

"How long have you been attending the book club?"

"About six months."

"How did Susan seem?"

"Her usual self. Happy. Laughing." Claire glanced from Bethany to Mike then back again. "I don't even know what I'm here for. I was just asked to pop down to help…"

"I'll tell you shortly. If we could just get the questions done first." Bethany smiled. "Now, do you know Susan well?"

"Only from book club and when I go in and pick up my reads or take them back. We have a chat and whatever. Has she done something wrong? I wouldn't know about anything like that—I mean, if she's dodgy. I mind my own."

"We're trying to determine whether she's done something to upset someone. Have you heard about a bad exchange or...?"

Claire shook her head. "No, like I said, I mind my own, and it's not like she's the sort to stand there telling you all her business. Well, apart from her recent tummy troubles."

"Tummy troubles?"

"The shits."

Oh. Nice. "So no one at the book club has been gossiping?"

"To be honest, I wouldn't have heard them anyway. I stick with Wendy and Rhiannon. We talk about general stuff for a bit before Susan starts the session, and from then on, it's the book, nothing more."

"Did everyone else seem happy enough last night?"

"As far as I could tell."

"What time did you leave?"

"I was the first one to go. I had to get back to let my pets out. I don't like them being cooped up inside for too long. So it would have been bang on ten or just after."

"Did you drive?" Bethany knew she had from CCTV but asked anyway.

"I did."

"Did you turn left or right out of the car park?" *To catch a lie.*

"Left. I live on the estate behind."

And she told the truth.

65

"Ah, that's helpful... You know the hedges at the back of the car park? The road you would have turned onto for the estate, those hedges would be to your left. Did you notice anyone standing there?"

"No, there's trees behind the hedges, lining the road."

Bethany could have kicked herself. Of course there was. She'd bloody stood under one with Mike while questioning Michele. "Did you see anyone at all on your drive home?"

"Only some kids messing about on their bikes, but that was in my street, and that's on the other side of the estate. I saw a few cars but didn't take any notice of them."

"Thank you for your time in coming here." She slid a card across the table. "If you think of anything, please give me a ring, and if I don't answer, phone the front desk. They'll get a message to me to call you back."

Claire rose. "You didn't say what this was about..."

"I'm very sorry, but Susan was murdered last night."

Down on her arse again, Claire leant back, her cheeks going white. "W-what? I don't...I can't... Susan?"

Bethany nodded. "It's a shock, isn't it?"

"I don't understand. She was lovely..."

Aren't they all... "So we're told, which is all the more frustrating for us. If everyone liked her, it makes it difficult to know why she was targeted.

My advice is to be careful at night. Don't go out alone, even if it's in your car."

Claire gulped. "Right. Um, yes, right..." She got up again and, clearly shaken, left the room.

"Penny, can you nip along and get the next one, please?"

Penny walked out and returned with a man, about fifty, slim, average height. He sat where Claire had, and Bethany looked down at the list of names.

"And you are?"

"Keith Crow."

She asked him the same questions, and he had no idea if anyone was upset with Susan either.

"So you said you left with your brother and gave him a lift." She glanced down at her pad again. "Evan. Did you take him straight home?"

"Yes, to the pub on the estate. The Grubby Basket."

The Grubby what...? "Okay, and how long did you stay there for?"

"Until chucking out time. Evan rents the flat upstairs. I kipped at his—had words with the missus earlier, and she said to keep out of her hair."

She queried him about the trees and hedges: *Did you see anyone there?*

He shook his head. "No, we were too busy laughing at something one of the other book clubbers said."

"And what was that?"

"Just that we're all worms, you know, bookworms, and it was funny, because during those words with my missus, she'd called me one an' all."

Was this anything to worry about? Was he the sort to do something like this if he was a worm? "In what way did she call you that?"

Keith shrugged. "You know, just a worm. She actually said: *Piss off out of my face, you fucking little worm.*"

"I see."

Mike coughed.

She asked Keith if he'd spotted anyone hanging around on the estate, and, like Claire, he'd only seen vehicles. Wrapping the interview up, she told him Susan had been murdered, and the smile was wiped from his face.

"You what?" He blinked several times. "After we'd left?"

Well, obviously… "Quite soon after."

"Blimey, so while we were downing pints, she was…"

"I'm afraid so. When you leave, can you stay away from the other room. We don't want anyone in there aware of what's happened until I tell them." She particularly meant his brother.

Next came Evan, then the others, and with none of them any help whatsoever, they were back to square one. Bethany and Mike traipsed to the incident room. Fran and Leona hadn't dragged anything of significance out either, neither had Talitia and Glen, and with a glance at the clock warning it was close to home time, she told them to pack up.

"I want you two with us tomorrow," she said to Talitia and Glen. "So eight o'clock, please, unless I call you in earlier." To Mike. "Fancy a pub meal?"

"The Grubby Basket, by any chance?"

She laughed. "You've read my mind.

She drove towards that estate. An officer stood at the library car park entrance.

"Just nipping in here a minute," she said and turned into it, showing her ID.

They signed the log, and she left the vehicle beside the SOCO van. The tent had gone, plus the body and Susan's car, but Isabelle was still there, on her hands and knees swabbing the chalk grid.

"Couldn't keep away?" Isabelle asked, peering up at them.

"We're just going for a working dinner," Bethany said. "Got anything else since we last spoke?"

Isabelle sighed, straightened up, and popped the swab in a tube, screwing the lid on. While she wrote on the label, she said, "Didn't Presley email you? He said he would."

Bethany checked her phone. "Nope."

"Bum, maybe his head's all up in the air because of his cat. I knew I should have done it myself."

"Come on, out with it. You know I don't like pratting about."

"Well, seems there's a gun involved."

"You'd better not be messing me around." Bethany's skin went cold.

"Not this time. What looks like the end of a gun had been put to the right side of Susan's head, at the temple. The imprint was hidden by her hair, so none of us spotted it first off. Pres managed to lift her—and let me tell you, seeing a rock-hard body being handled is *not* nice. He raised her top, and the same imprint was on her back. Now, that tells me it was pressed bloody hard for an imprint and a slight bruise to come up, plus, that must have been how they got her compliant."

"I did wonder." Bethany cringed. She'd sent everyone home, and they needed to run a check on gun licenses to see if any of the book clubbers or Richard Burrow and his sons had one. "What sort of gun is it?"

"He said a handgun but couldn't tell what sort. And he mentioned something about measuring the circle back at the morgue."

"Okay, thanks for that."

They left, and once she'd found a spot outside the pub, she sent a message to Rob on the front desk about guns, hoping he was still there. He wasn't, but Ursula Fringwell was. Bethany explained what was needed, and Ursula said she'd get the evening beat sergeant on it.

That sorted, they entered The Grubby Basket and approached the bar. Evan and Keith sat at the end on stools and waved. Greeting returned, Bethany ordered them a Coke each, and they chose a table out of the blokes' view and browsed the menu.

"So much for chatting to the manager about Evan and Keith," Mike said. "I gather that was your intention. Those two are going to be watching us now." He ran a finger down a list of food. "Steak for me. I'll pay for this."

She wasn't going to argue. "It's your turn anyway. I keep tabs."

He laughed. "I know you do. What are you having?"

"Chilli, please. Nachos, not rice."

While Mike went to the bar to order, she glanced around. A few people were eating, while others had clearly nipped in for a drink after work. Lots of shirts and suits about. Claire Billing entered with a man. It seemed the poor woman had been crying. Her companion led her to a table around the corner, and Bethany relaxed. While she loved her job, she could do with a break. It had been taxing, emotionally and mentally.

Mike returned and sat, a big grin in place.

"What's tickled your pickle?" she said.

"I was served by the manager and had a quiet chat. Keith and Evan were telling the truth—unless the landlord has already been told to lie for them. I believed him. He doesn't seem the type to suffer fools gladly."

"At least you got that out of the way. We can eat without worrying about it now. Claire Billing is in here."

Mike shrugged. "Yeah, I saw that. Maybe she needed a stiff drink after the news." He leant back, peering around the corner. "She's with a bloke. Nowhere near Keith and Evan."

"Well, if the three of them did it, they're hardly likely to be talking about it knowing we're here, are they, especially after Claire implied she only really knows Wendy and Rhiannon Tynen from the book club. I don't think it's any of that lot, by the way."

"Me neither." He sipped his Coke. "And I thought of something we didn't do."

"Shit, what?" She sighed.

"Talk to Susan's neighbours."

She could have screamed. Instead, she sighed. "We'll do it after dinner. Most people would have been at work earlier anyway. We're more likely to catch them in later."

They chatted for a bit, then their meals arrived. Halfway through eating, Bethany clocked Claire Billing and the man leaving. By the time they'd finished their food, Keith had walked out, and Evan strode past them to go through a door marked PRIVATE. None of them raised her suspicions.

Time wasn't stopping for anyone, so they made a move and arrived in Susan's street. Alice Jacobs' car was outside, so Richard must still be needing her support, although a FLO was also handy for listening to conversations within a family, watching reactions and behaviour, and determining whether they had anything to do with the crime in question.

Bethany and Mike split up, Mike doing the houses opposite, Bethany on the same side as Susan's. The closest neighbours had nothing but nice things to say, but four doors up was a different matter. An old man, closing in on eighty if she was any judge, ushered her inside so they could talk 'without some earwigging bastard listening in'.

In his living room, a sparse space with a walnut sideboard, an old, big-backed TV on a matching cabinet, and two floral, wooden-armed chairs, he got himself seated and lit a pipe. "She's a bloody jobsworth, that's what she is."

Bethany sat in the other chair. The scent of dust puffed up from the seat cushion, and the pipe smoke wafted over, bringing on thoughts of her late grandad. "Could you elaborate on that for me?"

"A stickler for the rules is Susan. If you're five minutes late bringing a bloody book back, she slaps on a fine."

"I thought so long as they were brought back on that day, it was okay."

"Huh, not with her new system. She's got it all on one of those newfangled computers, the exact time you took the book out, so say it was three o'clock, you need to get it back before three two weeks later. I was *six minutes* after three the other week, and she wouldn't back down. There another bloke there she did it to an' all, and he got a large levy, more than the usual. How ridiculous is that?"

73

"Sounds a bit over the top, I have to admit."

"She said it was because he was always late and he hadn't paid previous fines, so she added the twenty on top for 'interest', for God's sake. He could *buy* the bloody books with that. You go to that shop, The Works, and you get a fair few for that amount of money. They sell the sort of stuff he reads. Murder, he likes. Gruesome. I saw him holding a few of them that day."

That got her attention. "Do you know his name?"

"No, he's just a bloke to me."

Piddle. "Have you seen him there before?"

"No. I only go once a fortnight. Well, I say that, I stopped going because of Susan. I wait for the mobile library now. It stops outside our shops. And that Michele, she backed Susan up. The other woman who works there is nice, Vera, but she's only in on Thursdays, and I don't go out Thursdays."

She'd keep it in mind, what he'd said, but honestly, she couldn't see Susan being murdered over a fine. She paused the chat to send a message so someone could talk to this Vera. "Is there anything else you can tell me?"

"That's it. Isn't that enough? Can you sort it out so she loses her job now? That's why you're here, isn't it? Asking about her to see who she's annoyed?"

"No, sir. I'm afraid Susan was killed last night."

"Driving too fast, was she? I warned her about belting down the street. Ten miles an hour is too fast in my opinion."

Sounds like he's a jobsworth, too. Street patrol. "No, she was murdered."

He wafted smoke away from his face, seemingly not fazed by what she'd said. "The world's turned into a nasty place." He stuck his pipe in his mouth and sucked. Blew out. "Shame for Richard. He's nice. And their two sons—polite lads. But her? I've been told I can bear a grudge, and I suppose I can. I'll never forgive her for them fines."

Finally extracting herself from his home, Bethany chatted to the rest of the people on her side then sat in the car waiting for Mike.

"Get anything juicy?" he asked as he got in.

She told him about the old man. "Other than that, nothing but nice things said by everyone else."

"Same here. There's bugger all we can do tonight. May as well call it a day and crack on with it tomorrow."

She dropped him at his place then drove home. Sometimes, a long soak in the bath worked wonders. Oh, and a glass of wine.

CHAPTER SEVEN

Keith Crow stood waiting outside the old-fashioned red phone box that was now used as a free mini library. It was a good bit of community spirit, that, but most of the time it didn't have the sort of reads he liked, hence him using the main library. Still, he checked every week, and besides, he needed to wait for the alcohol to sod off out of his system. Wouldn't do to give his missus, Julie, something else to moan about, especially as she'd turfed him out last night. He should have bought some mints to disguise the smell so she didn't get a whiff.

He tapped his foot, hands in his jeans pockets. Old Bertram would be along in a bit with his donations—the bloke bought books off Amazon by the basket load and always dropped them here after he'd finished them. Keith aimed to get the pick of the bunch first. Normally, he was always too late.

I bet Susan's well dogged off about this little library.

He laughed, then remembered she was dead. Shit. He shouldn't be cracking up, not really. Susan was a nice bird. She'd given so many good recommendations for the book club that he selfishly wondered whether Michele or that other woman who worked there would select decent reads in the future. Vera, was it? Would there even be a book club now?

Mean of him to think like that. No wonder Julie had called him a worm.

Christ, where was Bertram? Maybe he'd decided not to come out tonight. It was nice and warm, a bit of lightness still in the sky, so perhaps he was giving it a miss, having a barbecue or whatever.

I'll give it ten more minutes, then I'm off to face Julie's music. Heavy metal in the form of a frying pan swung my way.

Keith didn't want to go home. Julie had an acid tongue on her, and she wouldn't hesitate in using it if she hadn't calmed down since yesterday. Blimey, he'd be better off just saying sorry, then everything would be okay. Until he fucked up again. Mind you, if he told her about Susan, it'd take the spotlight off him.

He nosed at his surroundings for something to do. A car came from the right, edging towards the top of the T-junction to Keith's left. Probably someone off to the nature reserve along the way there. As it drew closer, he worked out who it was. Bloody Zac Ferguson. He'd come here the past three weeks at the same time as Keith, waiting to pounce on Bertram for the crime books. It pissed Keith off, that did, because he liked those types of books an' all. He sighed, steeling himself to have a convo with Zac that he didn't want to have. The younger bloke was all right, just not Keith's cuppa. Word had spread that Zac now ran a money-lending racket, and Keith would be tempted if Zac didn't have that mad Erica and her hard-as-nails boyfriend doing the repayment collecting. They were a scary pair. Rumour had it she bumped people off if you paid her enough.

Had someone used her to kill Susan?
Fucking hell...

Zac parked but didn't get out like he usually did. The passenger window sailed down, and he leant across. "Bertram's been held up. Said to nip to his place if you want first dibs."

That was about a mile away, and Keith couldn't be arsed to traipse over there. "I'll leave it until next week." He turned to leave.

"Hop in, I'll take you," Zac called.

Hmm. Could he stand to be with Zac for the journey? The thing was, Keith got through a book a day, and he'd forgotten to take more out last night after the club—the row with Julie had seen him legging it from home rather than hanging about to collect the carrier bag containing the ones he'd already read. He'd get a bleedin' fine now.

Bollocks.

"Cheers." He got in the car and plugged the seat belt.

Zac smiled, zoomed the window up, clicked the locks—*strange*—then drove off. "Did you hear about Susan?"

"Yeah, been down the police station. They wanted to talk to everyone who was at the book club last night."

Zac turned right at the T. Odd. Bertram lived left, then left again.

"What did they ask?" Zac went a bit too fast, gripping the wheel, a total madman.

"'Ere, slow down a bit, will you?" Relieved when he did, Keith went on, "Oh, just if we saw anyone hanging about outside the library, that sort of thing."

"And did you?"

"Nope, me and Evan got in the car and went to The Grubby."

Zac nodded. "Anyone else see anything?"

"Dunno. Didn't speak to them about it. We didn't know why we were there until the copper told us during the interviews, and anyway, we had to leave after being spoken to—weren't allowed to chat to the others. Why are we going this way?" He didn't like Shadwell Hill, and that was where they were heading. Too many bodies had been found there, and it gave him the fucking creeps.

"Oh, Bertram's in the woods with his dog."

"But you said we had to go to his place."

"I forgot he messaged me to say the books are in his boot, so we're going there to meet him."

Fair enough. "What's the rush?"

"I need books. I can't be doing with using the library anymore. The rules are too bloody rigid. Susan slapped fines on like no one's business."

"Helps if you get them back on time..." Keith couldn't help the sarcasm. If you were late handing them in, what did you expect? You knew the rules when you signed up for a bloody library card. He'd be paying his without a murmur.

"You always were a snarky bastard." Zac turned left onto the track that led to the woods. "I'll never forget what you did to me when I was younger."

Keith frowned. He couldn't remember doing anything to him. "What are you going on about?"

Zac screeched to a halt in the car park. Bertram's vehicle wasn't there, and Keith grew uneasy. The air seemed to have thickened and buzzed with malice. Shit, he read too many crime books if he was thinking that way.

"Remember those lads who robbed that shop years ago?" Zac unclipped his seat belt and slid his hand into his lightweight jacket pocket.

"Yeah…"

"I was the one you grabbed hold of outside as the gang left."

Keith's guts rolled over. He thought back to that night. Winter. Ruddy cold. He'd nipped to the shop for a pint of milk and ten Bensons. Some kids had come rushing out, stupid masks on—animals, and one was a chicken—laughing and hooting about scoring a load of fags and Smirnoff, not to mention Bacardi Breezers and cash. Jesus, that had to be about fifteen years ago now, didn't it? And Zac was the kid he'd collared? Sodding Nora.

"I remember," Keith said. "You were a right little shit back then." He smiled.

"Dunno what you're smiling at, because I'm a right little shit now."

Keith glanced across at him.

Zac held a gun, and it pointed Keith's way.

Heart clattering, Keith opened his mouth to speak, but at the click of the trigger, the words dried up into husks on his tongue. What was going on? Was Zac *really* that annoyed about it—still? Keith had let Zac go back then, before the police had arrived, but had given him stern warning: "You ever do anything like this again, I'll fucking have you."

"You'll fucking have me," Zac said, as if reading Keith's mind. "I don't think so. *I'll* be having *you*."

Keith's insides went molten, and he scrabbled to undo his seat belt—then remembered Zac had locked the doors.

"Less of that." Zac waved the gun. "Unless you want your head blown off."

Zac was talking all weird, his voice funny—deep and eerie—and Keith stopped what he was doing. Stared. Couldn't think why Zac had waited all this time to do this. Why hold a grudge for so long? Surely now he was older he could see robbing your local shop wasn't on.

"Look." Keith held his hands up. "You don't need the gun. We can talk about this."

"Talking doesn't take the upset away. Susan found that out."

What? Oh fuck. Oh my God... "Susan...?" Keith blinked.

"Yeah, Susan. Now, we're going to sit here for a bit until it gets proper dark, then we're going to play a game."

A game? "W-what sort of game?"

"Tick, tack, toe."

"That's noughts and crosses. What are we playing *that* for?"

Zac grinned. "Because you deserve to lose."

Keith was getting on Zac's wick, shaking like that. Christ, what a muppet. Well, it'd serve him right. Poking his nose into Zac's business all those years ago had nearly cost him—if Keith hadn't let him go, Zac could've gone down for a stretch, seeing as it was 'armed' robbery. Funny, because he'd used the same toy gun that he pointed at Keith now. Okay, it was metal and looked the real deal, but it wouldn't fire any bullets.

"Keep still," Zac snapped. "You're doing my nut in, you bloody pleb."

Keith fidgeted, like he'd shit his pants or something. "We should talk."

"You should shut your gob."

"But what you did at the shop was wrong and—"

Zac pressed the gun to Keith's temple. Hard. "*Shut up!*"

"Oh God... What are you going to do to me?"

"Fuck me sideways, didn't you hear what I just said?" Zac shoved the gun forward so Keith's head smacked into the window. "You heard me cock this trigger, yet here you are, gassing. I could pull it any second, blow your head off, yet you feel the need to chat. It's best to just do as you're told from here on out, otherwise, Julie's going to get it."

"Please, please, leave Julie out of this."

Zac laughed and prepared himself to really go to town with The Voice of Fear. "You're in no position to tell me what to do, mate. If I want to go after Julie next, I fucking well will, got it?"

Keith nodded, lifting a hand to rub his bumped head. Zac kept a close eye on him—he wouldn't put it past the stupid bastard to lash out, try to move the gun away.

"Do as I say, and Julie stays safe," he all but growled. Funny.

Keith nodded. Whimpered.

Night crept in, full of stealth and the need to smother the daytime, a murderer just like Zac. He reckoned it was about time now. He kept the gun trained on his victim and pulled the keys from the ignition. The car park was ideal to draw the chalk grid on, what with it being smooth tarmac, the really black kind because the council had recently laid a new lot. He doubted anyone would come up here at this hour, and he'd sort Keith out in the far-left corner, so they'd be hidden by the trees that were like a curved arm around the car park, giving it a hug.

Laughter burbled inside him.

Don't lose it. Not until afterwards.

He got out and locked Keith inside. Asked himself if he could do this again.

Yes. Can't back out now.

At the boot, he stuffed the gun in his waistband, put on latex gloves, then took out his kill bag and carried it over to the corner. There, he laid his tools out, grabbed the chalk. Drawing the grid soothed him, and he marked two crosses in the first two top boxes, one for Susan, one for Keith. If the police had anything about them, they'd realise the rest of the boxes would also contain crosses by the time his spree was done.

Satisfied he had everything in order, he walked back to the car, thinking of Jambrea, out of it on the sofa. She'd woken earlier from the small amount he'd given her, saying she had a headache, and he'd muttered that he had one an' all, and it had the same name as her. She'd asked him what he'd said, and he'd replied, "Nothing."

Wouldn't hurt to let her think she was going a bit mental.

But that headache. Had the powder affected her brain already, like Lenny had said?

Those few grains had kept her asleep for three hours, so tonight, he'd put half a teaspoon in her wine—fuck the warning from Lenny. What did he know anyway?

Zac blipped the car doors unlocked and opened Keith's side. "Get out."

"W-what are you going to do to me?"

Zac yanked the gun out. "Just do as you're told, will you?" Ooh, he'd sounded well frightening then.

Keith obeyed, slowly exiting, hands up. They shook.

Good.

"Walk over there," Zac ordered, feeling all manly and shit. He could get used to this. Gone was the young lad who'd been forced to—

No. Concentrate on this, not back then.

Mercifully, thank the Lord and all the people in the Bible, Keith did as he was told, hands still up, and just because he could, Zac jabbed the gun in his back. Keith's "Ouch!"...*music to my lugholes, mate*.

"Now, get down on the ground. On your back." Another prod with the gun. He'd bet that was painful.

Keith went flying, landing on his knees. Was that a sob there? He bloody well should be sobbing for the trouble he could've caused on the robbery evening. Zac had had many a sleepless night as a teen, waiting for that knock on the door, coppers standing there ready to arrest him. Yeah, Keith needed to pay for that. You didn't go around scaring kids half to death, did you. Rude, that was. Unnecessary.

"Get on your back like I said," Zac snarled.

It was a bit difficult to see, so once Keith had finally done it, Zac switched his torch on low beam. It sliced across Keith's torso and face, showing the fear, how much he was bricking it.

"Please," Keith said.

"Please doesn't work with me. If you dog me off these days, that's it, end of story. Well, the end of yours anyway. This is your epilogue." Zac chuckled. "Did you like what I did there? We read books..."

"I just..."

"Shut it." He kicked Keith in the head. "Got nothing to *crow* about now, have you?" Now *that* was funny, playing around with Keith's surname.

"Heard that too many times to count," Keith ground out.

"What part of *shut it* don't you get? What part of being kicked in the head makes you think you can keep chatting shit? Susan did as she was told by this point, but you? Do I have to beat seven bells out of you or what?"

"Please…"

"That word is seriously wearing thin, you twonk."

Zac grabbed a cable tie, straddled Keith, and, after Keith slapped at him for a bit, Zac got him under control and secured his wrists together—not too tight so it left a mark, but then, his jacket sleeves would stop any rubbing.

"What… This is…" Keith's breathing had got a bit heavy. "I don't understand why…"

"Doesn't matter whether you understand or not, does it? This is where we are. This is the point we're at." Zac reached over for the scalpel. "Now for a bit of carving. I'm good at it. Won best Halloween pumpkin as a nipper." He stuffed a black rag in Keith's mouth—*ooh, the bastard tried to bite*—and got to work.

After the second slice, Keith blacked out.

Lightweight.

With no movement to mess up the tick, Zac was finished in no time, and he placed the skin in one of those plastic tubs you get your Chinese in. They were handy—never had to buy Tupperware again. Jambrea was pleased about that. He watched the blood run for a while, mesmerised by how it meandered down his temples, into his eyes, ears, and some finding its way to the creases in his neck.

Then he scooted backwards, sitting on Keith's thighs, and used his scissors to cut open the jacket and T-shirt, peeling the sides back. Fuck it. Keith had an outie belly button, so Zac couldn't wedge the toe in there.

To take his mind off that nuisance, he randomly pressed in the tacks, no pattern, no specific number. They took a bit of pushing, but each one finally popped in. Zac moved down to Keith's feet and took off his shoe and sock. He had a shorter second toe than Susan, and, using the cigar cutters from his kill bag, he lopped the little bugger off. Seeing as Keith was still unconscious, Zac took the time to use the scalpel on the toe. He ran the tip of it beneath the cut end of skin, loosening it from the flesh. Once that had been done all the way around, he peeled it back then clipped off the matter that was sticking out, creating a skin skirt. Perfect or what?

Back on Keith's thighs, he placed the toe base over the belly button then used tacks to hold the skirt in place. Now Keith looked just like Susan had, and Zac would need to take extra tacks next time in case the third victim also had an outie.

Talk about an inconvenience. Like he needed another trip to Rymans to buy more.

He sat and waited for Keith to wake up. Ten minutes passed. Bored, Zac popped his weapons inside a plastic carrier, then put them into the kill bag, which he dropped in the boot. May as well use the time wisely.

Car headlights, tiny between the trees, heralded a vehicle coming towards the area. Zac switched the torch off, breathing out in relief as the car sailed past, going towards the wind energy place up the way. Once the red taillights vanished, he flicked the torch back on.

Keith's eye were open. He groaned, the sound muffled behind the rag.

"Ah, deigned to join me, have you?" Zac stared down at him. Waiting, waiting for…

…the toe pain kicked in, and Keith bucked and writhed, a right old worm he was, his eyes bulging, his neck cords sticking out. He clenched his teeth, two rows of white gravestones, the rag bunched between them.

"Hurt, does it?" Zac stared at the belly button toe, sticking up and wiggling like some tiny little cock—ironic, because that was Keith all over. A tiny little cock who didn't deserve to live. "Ah, well, it'll be all over in a minute." Flexing his gloved hands to ensure they were limber, he straddled his victim again, reminding himself to remove the wrist and ankle bindings after. "Now, I'm going to strangle the fuck out of you, so keep nice and still, will you? I don't fancy a struggle tonight."

CHAPTER EIGHT

That bloody hill ought to be flattened, along with the woods. How many times had Bethany been called out to a body being discovered in that area? If it wasn't at Shadwell Hill, it was the woodland farther along, and to be honest, it was getting beyond a joke.

She'd thought people wouldn't go up there now the police drove past regularly, looking for vehicles late at night, people there to dump bodies. But no, someone had chosen it as a man's last resting place, and she was getting tired of seeing it. Not to mention seeing corpses.

She muttered obscenities on the way to the shower, hacked off at another early start. As Mike would say, it wasn't the victim's fault, and she reminded herself of that as she washed then got out. She dried, pulled jeans and a short-sleeved cotton shirt on in anticipation of another scorching day. If she could get away with wearing flip-flops she would, but instead chose a pair of black flats with fabric that allowed her feet to breathe.

She poured herself and Mike coffee in her to-go cups, grabbed a couple of Coco Pops breakfast bars—*not healthy, but bumholes to it*—and drove to Mike's. He waited on his path and waved, got in, and buckled up quickly so he could get some coffee down his neck.

"So what have we got then?" he asked as she drove away.

"What do you think? Same killer. Ursula said a dog walker found him."

"A *him* this time? Interesting."

"I thought that. As we've found in the past, when it's mixed sexes, it's usually personal."

"It's been personal when they're all the same sex as well."

"Whatever. Maybe I'm looking for something to hang on to." She could have blushed at her mistake but didn't allow the emotions that created one to affect her. "I'm talking out of my arse. Happens from time to time."

"Blame it on the early hour. You usually do." Mike smiled.

"Get lost, you cheeky git. So, we're off to the that bloody hill again."

"You've got to admit, it's an ideal place to leave bodies. Easy. Out of the way."

"I know, but I'm sick of going up there. And before you say it, yes, I'm sure the victim was sick of being up there as well."

"Any ID?"

"Nicola Eccles and Penny Dickens are there. They didn't touch anything and are waiting for Isabelle and her lot to arrive. Want a Coco Pop bar?" She gestured to the glove box.

Mike leant forward and got two out. "I assume that was you saying you wanted one, and can I open it for you."

"Might have been." She took the proffered food. "Ta."

They munched in silence, and by the time they'd finished, Shadwell Hill loomed to the left, the sky a bright blue at six in the sodding morning. The curve of trees hid any activity and would do so until they drove up the track and entered the car park. She did that, the track long and on an incline and, at the top, she came to a stop behind the patrol car on the far right. Another vehicle, a blue

Fiat, sat in the middle, and a woman was in the driver's seat, side-on so her feet were outside, her head between her legs. Nicola stood with her, while Penny was in the top-left corner by what appeared, from this distance, to be a mound.

"Someone feels sick then," Mike said.

"Shame. It's awful and we're used to it, so God knows what it's like for civvies."

Bethany and Mike got out, and a rather excited black-and-white dog bounded about on the Fiat's back seat, coming to the window to press a wet nose to the glass, the daft bugger.

"Morning," Bethany said.

The woman lifted her torso and stared up at her. Red-rimmed eyes—they all had them, the finders—and mottled cheeks. She was fit, going by her lean body and running gear.

"DI Bethany Smith, and this is DS Mike Wilkins." She held up her ID. "And you are?"

"Roslynn Ernst."

"You were walking your dog, I take it?" Bethany smiled, saddened that this lady had come here for a morning run and now her whole day—and the rest of her life—would be tainted by someone else's wicked actions.

How cruel it was, that another human could wreck your world—by choice. How unforgivable that they had the power to do so, their actions giving life sentences.

Roslynn nodded. "But we didn't go running. I saw...saw that lump over there and wondered what it was. I jogged over and..." She shivered.

"Don't worry about explaining that, I'll see for myself in a moment. I want to know what you did once you were there."

"I screamed and backed away."

"So you didn't touch anything?"

"No, I didn't get that close either. Once I saw it was a body, and there was blood…"

"Okay. Then what?"

"I came back to the car and got in, locked the doors. I was scared someone was out there, watching from the woods. Then I called the police. They came quickly, thank God, because I wasn't going to sit here for long if there's a killer about."

"Understandable. You say you didn't get close. Did you see the face at all?"

Roslynn bobbed her head and clutched her hands in her lap. "Just that it was a man and he had red lines on his forehead."

The tick… "So you didn't recognise him?"

"No. I… I haven't lived in Shadwell long. I only know the people at work and my next-door neighbours. I expect that'll change soon because I've joined the yoga class at the sports centre. I start next week."

"Where do you live?" Bethany glanced across at Mike, who had his notebook ready.

"On the Ring Road estate." She gave the exact address.

Oh. That wasn't a nice place. A high-rise. Full of drug runners and undesirables.

"I can see by your face what you think of that," Roslynn said, "but I didn't know what it was like there until I came. My work rented the flat for me. I'm originally from Cirencester. I plan to move. I don't...the place scares me a bit. It doesn't feel right."

"There are a few good roads there." *If you don't mind pushers on your street corner.* Bethany looked at the dog, who'd pressed his nose so hard on the glass that it bent to one side. She wanted to laugh at the silly sod but held it in. Not appropriate. "What time did you arrive here this morning?"

"Half five."

"That's pretty early for a woman to be out alone." Bethany frowned. "Shadwell isn't... Let's just say it's not safe these days. It would be advisable not to come up here at all—or to the woods along the way a bit. You might not have heard about what it's like here while you lived in Cirencester. Trust me, find somewhere else to run. You can go home now. And is there anyone you could call to sit with you for a bit?"

Roslynn nodded. "Yes, my neighbour. And she told me all about the murders here lately—so many of them over the past couple of years. I wish I'd never come, but I'm bound by a two-year contract. The money was too good to pass up."

Bethany sighed. "It's a city. There are always murders, you just don't get to hear about the majority of them—unless the local paper gets involved or there's a press conference." She wondered whether Uxbridge had written a story about Susan yet and how long it would be before his police informant leaked the news of this one.

"Okay, so you're fine to drive?" At the woman's nod, she handed Roslynn her card. "If you feel you need some support, ring the station and tell them DI Smith said Alice Jacobs can come and see you. She's the liaison officer."

I need to find out whether Alice ended up staying the night at Susan's.

"Thank you." Roslynn swung her legs inside the car and closed the door.

Bethany, Mike, and Nicola stepped back. Roslynn drove away, the dog barking as if to say: *Oi, you didn't let me have my run!*

"Let's pop some tape held down by evidence markers to show where she parked," Bethany said.

Nicola got busy with that while Bethany walked over to her car and sorted protective clothing. Once she and Mike were kitted out, she led the way to Penny, who held the scene log for them to sign.

"Bit of a shit start to the day, eh?" Bethany said.

Penny took the log off Mike then gave it to Bethany, who scribbled her name and the time.

"Just a bit." Penny peered over Bethany's shoulder while taking the log off her. "SOCO are here."

Bethany faced the road, peering round the tree curve. The van trundled along then veered onto the track. Bethany and Mike went to meet it, waiting by her car. She waved at the driver to come over, and he parked.

Isabelle jumped out of the back. "Morning! Might have known this would be a serial—bet you it is. One more, and we're really under pressure." She gawked over, eyes widening at the body. "Tent over there, please. And be quick about it, there's another bloody vehicle coming."

"Nicola?" Bethany shouted. "Turn them away, please. But ask if they saw anything first, will you?"

Nicola waved and headed to the track.

"Actually, once you've dealt with them, go down to the road and get rid of people from there. Ring the front desk and tell Ursula I want another uniform—Tory, not Talitia or Glen." *I need them with Fran and Leona, thank you*.

SOCOs carried the tent equipment across to Penny and got on with setting up.

"Same as before, is it?" Isabelle asked.

They took a slow walk over to the scene.

"Can't say I looked at the body," Bethany said, "but it sounds like it."

"Yep, same MO," Mike said. "Although this time, they tacked the toe in place."

Bethany's stomach rolled over. The Coco Pop bar hadn't been such a good idea. "Oh, for God's sake."

"The chalk grid has a second cross in it, but we anticipated that, didn't we," he said.

They came to a stop and nattered about anything and everything to pass the time. With the tent in place, Isabelle entered first. The photographer was already hard at it, clicking away with his camera. Isabelle ran a well-oiled machine with her team, and they all worked without being instructed. Most of the time, Bethany thought Isabelle issued orders just so she felt she was doing something constructive.

"This is just the weirdest thing," Isabelle said, staring at the body.

"Oh, hang on a minute…" Mike stepped closer. "I didn't twig before, what with the blood, but is that Keith Crow?"

"Keith who?" Isabelle frowned.

Bethany jolted. "What, *our* Keith Crow?" Shit, she'd have to look at the body faster that she would've liked. First Susan, now Keith. Was it something to do with the library? It had to be, didn't it? "Shit, two seconds." She whipped her phone out and, cursing the fact she'd have to get her team in early again, contacted Leona.

Bethany: ANOTHER BODY. KEITH CROW. CAN YOU GET INTO WORK AND CONTACT ALL THE BOOK CLUBBERS, WARNING THEM TO BE CAREFUL? DON'T CALL EVAN, THOUGH. HE MIGHT NOT BE THE NEXT OF KIN, SO I'LL FIND OUT WHO THAT IS FROM URSULA AND GIVE THEM A VISIT BEFORE HE GETS TOLD.

Leona: OKAY. BEFORE I FORGET, VERA IS IN THE CLEAR. WHERE IS THE BODY?

Bethany: SHADWELL BLOODY HILL, SO CCTV IS GOING TO BE A LOAD OF SHIT, BUT YOU NEVER KNOW, YOU MIGHT GET LUCKY AND COME UP WITH A NUMBER PLATE OF SOMEONE HEADING IN THIS DIRECTION. I DON'T KNOW WHEN HE DIED YET, PRESLEY ISN'T HERE, SO LOOK AT FOOTAGE FROM ABOUT SIX LAST NIGHT, ALTHOUGH IT WOULD HAVE STILL BEEN LIGHT. GET GLEN AND TALITIA IN EARLY

TO HELP YOU. FRAN CAN COME IN AT HER USUAL TIME.

Leona: ON IT. I'LL BE AT WORK IN ABOUT FIFTEEN MINS.

Bethany: THANKS.

Then she rang Ursula for the next of kin, and as it happened, it was Evan.

Keith had mentioned having a row with his girlfriend, so they'd have to visit her afterwards. If they could get that done inside an hour and a half, they could return here. By that time, Presley would be on the scene.

"Right, we're going to shoot off," she said. "Back as soon as we can."

They took off their protectives, and she drove them to The Grubby Basket. Parked, she caught sight of a door she hadn't noticed last time. The pub would be shut, but what if that was the one used by staff? Someone had to be in there, maybe prepping food. She walked over, Mike by her side, and rang the bell, which jangled out a bizarre, strangled buzz that sounded like the batteries needed changing. She peered through the glass rectangle in the top half. Stairs with cream lino, the riser edges capped with steel, and a short hallway in front of them. Socked feet appeared at the top, then suit trousers, a bare torso, and finally, Evan's face topped with damp hair. He frowned, approaching the door with his hand out ready to twist the latch. The hairs on his fingers were well thick.

"Yes?" He held the door wide with his foot, some cartoon character's lips the toe end of his sock.

She wondered if he had boxers on to match. "May we come in?"

"What for? I told you all I knew yesterday."

"We know you did. It's about Keith."

His eyebrows fled up his forehead as if wanting to hide in his hairline. "Don't you be coming round here and telling me he did Susan in, because that's bollocks. He was with me that night, and I said that in the interview."

Bristling much?

"We really do need to come in," Mike said.

"Bloody hell. What's happened? Has he had another barney with Julie or what? Has she reported him?" He walked off and climbed the stairs.

Inside, Bethany closed the door, and up in the flat, they had to walk around in order to find him. He was in a bedroom, doing up a blue shirt in front of a free-standing pine mirror.

"I don't want anything to do with their arguments," he went on, as if there hadn't been a break in conversation. "She's a right picky cow, if you want the truth, always getting at him. The bloke can't breathe and she's on at him. I've told him to move out and share the rent of this place, there's a spare bedroom, but he won't have it. Says he loves her." He tucked his shirt in. "Personally, I think she's just after him for his money. He earns a fair whack." Tie grabbed, he slung it around his neck—a neck growing redder by the second.

"Can you just sit on the bed for a moment," Bethany asked.

"Sit on the bed? I've got to get to work."

"Sit," Mike said, no-nonsense.

Blimey, he's being forceful today.

Evan flopped down and stared at Mike defiantly. "Just get on with it, will you?"

Mike glanced at Bethany: *Rip the plaster off now or ask questions first?*

She stared back: *Plaster.*

"I'm sorry to have to tell you this," Mike said, "but Keith was found dead this morning."

Evan fell backwards on the crumpled quilt and stared at the ceiling. "W-what?" He shot upright again. "Was it Julie? Did she go for him? I warned him she was a bit of a nutter, but he wouldn't listen. Fuck. *Shit!*"

"No, it wasn't Julie, as far as we're aware," Bethany said. "We think it was the same person who killed Susan Burrow." She let that sink in for a moment.

Evan's face writhed from a multitude of emotions, one after the other: disbelief, confusion, fear, and lastly, sorrow. She waited for him to cry it out. He rocked back and forth, hands covering his face, muttering that everyone was gone now, just him left, and what was he supposed to do without his big brother? A good five minutes passed like this, then he composed himself, dropped his hands to his lap, and cleared his throat.

"Sorry. I'm sorry," he said.

"Please don't apologise for grief," she said.

"Yeah, but it can't be nice for you." He wiped his cheeks.

Not in my job and not in my life, but we have to learn to live with it, accept it, and move on. Vinny's warm laughter echoed somewhere, in her head, her heart, she didn't know, but she took comfort from it. He was there with her still, even though she couldn't see or touch him. That would have to be enough for the rest of her days. Evan would learn to do the same. It might not be the existence she or Evan had envisaged, but it was their reality.

"It's okay," she said. "We'd rather you cry than bottle it all up." *But bottling it up helped me. Pretending it didn't happen, that I'm not alone, that I hear my dead husband's voice, feel him close by.* "Sorry to ask questions when you've just had terrible news, but when was the last time you saw Keith?"

"In the pub yesterday. You were here; I saw you. We waved, remember? He left, then I came upstairs."

Yes, she remembered. "Do you know where he was going?"

"Yeah, to the free library."

"And where is that?"

"On the edge of the estate. I'll show you; can't recall the name of the road it's on." He took his phone out, jabbed at Google, then handed her his mobile. A map. "Just there." He pointed.

Mike leant over and wrote down the street name. "Was he going to the free library because the usual one wasn't open?"

"No, he was going up there to meet Bertram."

"Who's that?" Mike asked.

"Some old fella who donates crime books, thrillers and stuff like that."

"Do you know where he lives?" Bethany handed the phone back.

"Yeah, over the shop, the Tesco Express."

"On this estate?"

"Yes."

"Okay, thank you. And could we also have Julie's address?" She had it somewhere back at the station from when she'd first spoken to Keith, but it was no good to her there.

Evan reeled it off, and Mike wrote it down.

"Was he going home after that?" She thought about Keith making himself scarce once Julie had called him a worm—the woman might have thought he'd stayed away longer than just one night and had no cause to worry.

"Yes, and he said if Julie was iffy with him, he'd come back here. He didn't. Obviously." His face crumpled again, and a sob choked out.

After making sure he'd be all right, they left him to pick up the broken pieces their visit had created. She drove them to the Tesco Express next—it was more important to visit the book man who may have seen Keith than break the news to Julie.

"Unfortunately, I didn't donate any books last night," Bertram said. "I had someone call round to collect a few, we had a cup of tea, then I fell sleep. Woke up at midnight. Couldn't believe I'd napped like that."

"Who came round?"

"Zac Ferguson. Bit of a jack the lad, but he doesn't bother me. He took about four novels then buggered off."

There was nothing left but to visit Julie. Bethany steeled herself for that. Telling two people bad news in one day never boded well.

CHAPTER NINE

"Give me strength! Shut them the hell up, will you?" Lenny slammed his cup down on the kitchen island. Coffee sloshed over the sides and dribbled on his meaty fingers.

Erica stared at him, anger stirring. "You would do well not to speak to me that way." She gave him a stare that said: *Do you want me to break your neck?*

He glared back, a faint tic by his eye. Good, she'd got her message across. For all his brawn, he was afraid of her. She'd once told him she'd strangled a boyfriend while he'd slept, then threw his body in a Russian river. This admission helped to keep her boyfriend in line.

He grabbed a tea towel and wiped his hand, then the island. "Look, they're going to get the neighbours nosing, making that sort of racket."

She snorted. The cheek of him. "That is not my fault. You can deal with them. They are nothing to do with me."

"But they're scared of me."

"Is it any wonder?" She scowled. "You punched one of them. They are terrified. In a strange country. Who knows where they are going next." This wasn't her responsibility. Wasn't her line of business. She frightened people into paying up, killed someone if they deserved it—for a price. She didn't offer illegal immigrants a bed for the night—or in this case, the floor. The job was Lenny's. Still, he helped her with collections, so perhaps she'd do as he wanted. For now. "Next time, do not order me. Ask nicely. Say: *Erica, please quieten the guests.* And this had better not happen again. This is *my* house. I do not want business here. The rule is jobs are never brought indoors in case police come. And that includes your drugs. Get them out. Store them elsewhere."

She strode from the kitchen, giving him the middle finger over her shoulder for the shitty look he was probably levelling at her. She didn't love him, he was a man who happened to fit her current needs, so if they fell out, he could walk. There were plenty of Lennys around. Men liked women who could crack a walnut between their thighs, so she'd heard. She'd find someone else easily.

Erica went upstairs to the large spare bedroom at the back and unlocked the door. The stench hit her first—too many bodies, too much bad breath, unwashed skin, gasses. If she didn't have a strong stomach, she'd be sick, but she'd smelt worse—a rotting corpse she'd gone back to visit when the police hadn't found it. She'd left it in a prominent position for them, too.

Lenny had fitted wood across the windows using nails in the frame, the bloody maggot. Well, *he* could fix any damage. He'd also removed all the furniture—the queen-sized bed, white vanity table, and the Edwardian-style chest of drawers. She'd bet he'd crammed them into the other spare room. He must have done it while she was out yesterday. He hadn't confessed to the guests being there until this morning, after they'd been installed and had made a noise.

Fucker.

Several faces stared at her. Young, skinny men, still bearing the muddy marks put on their cheeks to camouflage them on their walk through the countryside last night where they'd stopped at a prearranged spot. They'd waited for Lenny to pick them up in the van he'd borrowed, heads probably full of dreams of a better life, full bellies, and money in their pockets. Lenny had confessed this after she'd grabbed his bollocks and twisted them.

Their clothes needed a good wash, all but rags, hanging off their emaciated frames. He said they'd 'come in off the boat', and she'd known, then, exactly what he was involved in. Their wrists had been tied behind them. Rope.

Stupid. She would have used metal cable ties.

"Shh," she said, frowning. "You are too noisy."

"Hungry and need the bathroom," one of them said in broken English, the ceiling bulb reflected in his irises, two moons in pools of shite.

For fuck's sake... "One at a time. You." She pointed to the speaker. "Try anything, I crack your spine."

He managed to get to his feet and jerked his head to indicate his bonds.

"What," she said, "you want me to hold your dick? Sit on the toilet. I will not touch your dirty sausage or bulbous plums." She shivered inwardly.

He sidled past her as though he thought she might actually crack his spine, and she tilted her chin to let him know where he needed to go. In he went, and the door closed.

The others stared at her, begging with their eyes. *Food, we need food.*

Damn her heart. A small part of it, the bit she reserved for when she was a normal human, which wasn't often, twanged. She'd send Lenny out for McDonald's. They'd have to eat like cats and dogs, on their hands and knees—she wasn't releasing their wrists. While she could subdue every one of them inside ten seconds if they had a mind to attack her should she untie them, she didn't want to.

The first man returned, shuffling along, his trousers round his ankles.

"You will have to ask your friends for help with those," she said.

One by one, they used the toilet, then she locked them up again, thinking of the struggle they'd have trying to pull each other's kecks up. Through the door, she called, "I will get food. Now shut up until it arrives. You, the one who spoke English. Translate that to the others. Any noise, I will blame you. Kneecap you. Smash your ribs. One kick, one punch. Do you understand?" And there she'd been, telling Lenny off for frightening them.

A muffled 'yes', then a sob.

She didn't need to hear that. It almost had her setting them free. "Good. Now silence!"

She cleaned the toilet, shuddering at the idea of filthy bums on the seat. The sink and bath got a good going over, too, just in case they'd touched them.

Downstairs, she caught Lenny rubbing his crotch while looking at his phone.

"Perverted creature," she snapped. "Your guests need food. They are hungry. I have just done their toilet break. You. McDonald's. Get out and do it now. They had better be gone by tonight, like you said. The room smells like feet. You can buy me a Yankee Candle to burn in there once they've left. Baby Powder. My favourite. Do not forget."

He stood, shoved his phone in his pocket, and walked up to her. Cupped her cheek. Kissed her nose. "This'll send us on a nice holiday. Five grand to keep them upstairs until later. Not a bad bit of work, eh?"

"Piss off for the Big Macs. The fries. The breakfast menu has finished now. Get them apple pies. And milkshakes."

"Give us the dosh then."

"That will be a large fuck off to you. Leave."

Lenny laughed and walked out.

That bastard. She'd have to trade him in for another model, no matter how handy he was on money collection night. Until she found someone else, she'd have to put up with him. Then she'd strangle him and throw him in an *English* river.

Jambrea was getting on Zac's nerves again. If she didn't watch it, he'd lump her one. How often had he thought that recently? How could he cope with her whinging when he had important things on his mind? Why did she have to query everything he was doing lately? Or had she always done it, and he only noticed now because she might catch on to what he was up to and dob him in?

The questions were doing his head in.

"But it hurts," she wailed, draping her arm over her eyes. Sprawled on the sofa the way she was, it looked like she was pissed, one too many tequilas infiltrating her blood.

"It's just a headache, woman," he said from the chair by the door. *Unless that stuff's attacking your brain.* He gave the TV his attention. One of those bugging Nationwide adverts was on, the one about Monopoly—*can't afford that, can't afford that...* Christ, who thought them up? "You're probably coming down with something. Summer flu."

"But it's a big migraine. I need co-codamol."

Blimey, it must be bad if good old paracetamol wasn't going to cut it. "We don't have any."

"Then go and get some, you dopey prick."

Oh. He could just ball his fist now and— "Right. Right. Keep your fucking wig on."

He stormed out, slamming the door, laughing at the thought of her wincing or, most likely, screeching in pain. He nipped to Boots, parking on double yellows, and had to make out to the nosy-as-eff pharmacist that the tablets were for him— "Got a dodgy hip, haven't I..."—then got back in the car.

He didn't want to go home.

Some dick had borrowed money off him this morning—covert meeting round the back of Tesco Express, here's the cash, collector will be round next week, and if you don't cough up, she'll shiv you, dickface.

He could do with letting Erica know.

Zac detoured round there, sod Jambrea and her manky noggin. He pulled up out the front. Waited for the blank eye to appear in the blinds. It didn't, so he gave a quick bip on the horn. Erica swung the door open and marched down the drive, fluffy slippers something he hadn't imagined her in. For some reason, he'd thought she'd have opted for those ones with kitten heels like they had in the fifties or whatever.

Window down, he waited for a good look at her dough balls again.

She shoved her head inside. "What do you want? I cannot have you keep coming here like this." A furtive glance at her house, then back to him.

No tits on show. The neckline was too high. Bollocks.

"You said not to text information," he said. "You told me to speak in person about work."

"You know you can text and ask for a date so we can speak. This was agreed—this lets me know you need to talk. If people get hold of our phones, it looks like we are seeing each other. You know, a date-date." She peered up and down the street. Back to him again, eyes icy.

The way she was bent over, he'd give anything to be standing behind her. Her rump, like a peach it was, except he'd bet it wasn't furry. It'd be all smooth and—

"Why are your eyes glazed?" she whisper-shouted. "Are you on Lenny's capsules?"

"Capsules?"

114

She glared at him. "You know what I am talking about."

"Um, no, I'm not on anything. Listen, I have another customer." He scribbled the name and address on an Argos receipt he found in the glove box, the one for the safe. "Five hundred each repayment for six weeks."

She snatched it. "Right. Now go away. And remember, ask for a date next time."

He only wished it'd be a real one.

She straightened, smoothed down her top, and strutted off.

That arse…

He drove away before anything went on in his boxers. A van headed towards him, and the wanky driver hogged most of the road between parked cars either side, so Zac had to idle to let him pass.

Lenny glared at him through the windscreen, stopped, and lowered his window. "What are you doing round here?"

"Dropping off client info." *What the fuck's it got to do with you?* "I was in the area."

"Well don't. You know the score."

"Yeah, yeah. By the way, thanks for the gear you gave me." Zac nodded knowingly. "Works a treat."

"Getting sleep hasn't done much for your face. A bag full of hammers, it is." Lenny sped off, laughing.

"Gimp." Zac went home. Grabbed Jambrea's meds. Inside, he was greeted with the sound of her sobbing. "That's not going to help your headache." He threw the paper bag on her stomach,

115

wondering if the co-codamol would react with the 'gear' still in her system. Deciding he didn't give much of a monkey's, he got her a bottle of water from the fridge and took it in to her.

She'd managed to sit up and held two tablets in her palm.

"Get those down your neck." He lobbed the bottle on the sofa. It bounced then rested on her elbow. "Maybe you'll stop moaning in about ten minutes once they've kicked in."

"Why are you so horrible to me?" she said, opening the water and giving him evils.

"I'm not getting into why." He left the room so he didn't have to explain.

Not yet. Not until the night he killed her.

Then she'd know why.

Jambrea closed her eyes for a few minutes. The tablets were working wonders already, the pain receding, her mind clearing. Something wasn't right, though, and not just with her head either, which had felt as though her brain was being boiled. Zac wasn't the same these days, acting all weird and snappy, or vacant, like he was miles away. Was he thinking about another woman? That Erica?

She huffed out a breath.

Course of action decided, because she wasn't going to get a straight answer from Zac, she pushed herself off the sofa and, ignoring him in the kitchen, went upstairs for a shower. Much more refreshed afterwards, she put on her running outfit so he'd think she was off for her usual jog. At the front door, she slid a key and her phone into her Lycra leggings pocket, zipped it closed, and turned the Yale.

"Oi, where are you going?" Zac called. "Thought you had a bad head."

She didn't face him. He'd see the lie in her expression. "Running, what's it look like?"

She walked out and took off up the street.

On the other side of the estate, she stood in Erica's road, out of breath, hot, but her skull free from agony at last. She felt fine now—so much for Zac's prediction of summer flu, the pillock—and waited for a bit so she didn't appear a sweaty mess when she confronted Miss Perfect Tits.

Five minutes later, she was on her doorstep, ringing the bell. Erica opened up and stared, appearing as though she'd self-combust any second. The waft of Big Macs floated out, and Jambrea remembered she hadn't eaten yet. That explained the migraine.

"What do you want?" Erica said.

"We need to talk."

"About?" Erica drummed her nails on the doorframe.

"Zac."

Erica snooped up and down the street. "This is more trouble than it is worth. I do not earn enough from him to put up with this shit. Get inside."

Jambrea went in, and Erica shoved her in the back to hurry her up, then slammed the door.

"What was that for?" Jambrea asked, righting herself so she didn't stumble into the newel post.

"I can do worse. Fractures, breaks, bruises. Death." Erica shrugged. "Take your pick."

Jambrea didn't feel so confident now she was in the woman's home, but it was too late. She was here—and she wanted answers. She shoved aside the fact that Erica was possibly a killer and got on with the matter at hand. "No, thank you. Violence isn't necessary."

"You would be surprised how much it is." Erica, the mysterious, freaky cow, led the way to the kitchen. "Sit. You cannot have coffee. You are not staying long."

Lenny came in from the conservatory out the back. "What do *you* want?"

What was it with everyone talking to her like this? "Nothing to do with you." Jambrea didn't like him. He gave her the jitters.

"Piss off," Erica said to him. "Ladies' business."

Lenny backed away. "Right." He went into the conservatory and closed the door.

"Now, spit out your words, then leave," Erica demanded.

"Are you shagging Zac?" There. She'd said it. Her heart throbbed, and she needed a wee.

"Why would I want to do that?" Erica's face—expressionless.

"Well, he's a bit of a catch."

118

"Like fish? Are you saying he looks like cod? Why would I shag cod?"

This wasn't going at all like Jambrea had imagined. "No, I'm not saying that. So, are you doing him or what? That's all I want to know."

"I am not. He is not my type. Lenny is, which is why he services me. Now go home." Erica pointed to the kitchen door.

"Can I use your loo?" Jambrea asked. "Then I'll be on my way."

"Top of the stairs. Be quick."

"Thanks." She shot up there, instead going into the bedroom that had the door open. A double bed. Erica's perfumes on a chest of drawers. A makeup brush balanced on a pot of bronzer. What did she expect to find, Zac's underwear? Feeling stupid, and desperate for stooping so low, she went to the toilet, just so she could flush it and Erica wouldn't know she'd been nosing. When she came out, a *donk* thudded from her left, then a muffled shout.

She inched her way to the door. Was someone in there? An old-fashioned filigree key sat in the lock. There was that *donk* again, another voice. She twisted the key and peered inside. The smell... Big Macs and stale cheese. Body odour. She gagged, holding her hand over her mouth, then registered people.

Men. Dirty. Staring at her.

"What are you doing, you stupid little bitch?"

Erica. Behind her.

Jambrea spun round, and Erica shoved her in the chest. Jambrea went sprawling backwards into the room, arms windmilling, legs going from under her. She landed on a skinny bloke and scrambled off him, whimpering, and shuffled on her arse to the radiator. Leaning against it, she stared from the other occupants to Erica in the doorway.

"Now look what you have done," Erica said.

"What's going on?" Jambrea tried to stand, but fear crept in, sending her body to jelly.

"What is going on? You, being a detective. Coming here, accusing me of tasting your fish, then looking into things you should not be looking into. You should have just gone home." She gave a chilling stare. "What do you have in your pocket?"

"M-my phone. A k-k-key."

"Give the phone to me."

Jambrea got it out, and Erica stepped forward to snatch it away.

"Lenny!" Erica shouted.

He appeared inside a minute.

"Your gear," Erica said. "She needs some."

"Oh, fuck me. How did this happen?" He gawped at Jambrea.

"It does not matter, it is done." Erica eyed them all one by one. "In fact, give everyone the gear. It was them being noisy that caught Thelma's attention."

Who is Thelma?

Lenny seemed to have the same query. "Thelma?"

"From *Scooby Doo*, you bloody dense gobshite. I watch it since I moved here." Erica sighed.

And gear? What is she on about?

Jambrea soon found out. Lenny disappeared then came back with a plastic beaker of water. He handed it to her and ordered her to swallow the lot. She did, too afraid of them both to do anything else. Then that woozy feeling came over her, like it had yesterday with her cup of tea and the drink Zac had given her last night. Just as she fell asleep, she realised she'd been drugged. Then: *These men... Who are they? And why are they locked inside Erica's spare bedroom?*

CHAPTER TEN

Julie wasn't what Bethany had expected. The woman stood in the doorway, rail-thin, looking like she'd stepped out of a fashion magazine, all latest trends and beautiful, straight blonde hair. She didn't seem the sort to call her boyfriend a worm, but first impressions could be deceptive little devils, full of promise, when in reality, trickery lurked in the shadows. Those kind blue eyes of hers could turn cruel any second, showing Bethany how mean Julie really was underneath it all. Or maybe Evan saw her how he wanted to, perhaps jealous his brother had a girlfriend and he didn't. Keith may well have played up how she behaved so he got sympathy from Evan. Who knew?

"DI Bethany Smith, and my partner, DS Mike Wilkins. We're here about Keith. Can we come in?" She held up her ID.

Julie eyed them warily then, her perfect façade slipping, the top layer peeling back to expose the potential infected ones beneath. People were onions.

"What's he done?" The voice didn't match the appearance. A tad abrasive on the old ears, like she was too fond of Lambert and Butler or had recently shouted a fair bit. "Got drunk with his brother and caused trouble, has he? I warned him Evan is a piece of work, would lead him down the garden path *and* around the corner, but will he listen? No." She released a long breath. "Come in. I was just about to do a drop-in at the salon for a trim, but I can go later. Trust Keith to balls that up as well."

Bethany glanced at Mike: *Bloody hell*…

Julie waited for them to enter, then closed the door and took them into the living room— minimal, grey and black, a couple of white ornaments, chrome this and that. "Want some tea?"

Bethany shook her head. "Thanks, but no." She gestured to the sofa for Julie to sit. Once she had, she asked, "When was the last time you saw Keith?"

Julie looked up at her, a smug smile in place. "That's easy. The night before last. We had a row, and I told him get out of my face. He'd pushed my buttons one too many times, and I'd had enough. Don't you want to sit down, too?"

Bethany chose a steel-coloured suede armchair, which was almost invisible, what with the amount of throw cushions on it. Sitting there was uncomfortable, so she perched on the edge and hoped she didn't slip off. Mike remained standing, ready to take notes, unsuccessful in hiding his smile at Bethany's predicament, the sod.

She gave him a *don't you dare laugh* look then addressed Julie. "What was the row about?" She hoped that wouldn't set the woman off. She wasn't in the mood for histrionics. The two early starts this week had wreaked havoc with her ability to engage the patience gene.

"Why do you need to know *that*?" Julie narrowed her eyes and leant back against a bundle of fluffy pillows, the oversized kind. She crossed her ankles and rested her hands in her lap.

"Please just answer the question." Bethany smiled. Tightly. *Don't mess me about, love. Not today.*

Julie sighed, dramatic fashion ahoy. "Oh, all right then, even though it isn't any of your business." Her features crimped into an expression of contempt.

I can see exactly what Evan means.

"I think you'll find it is her business, otherwise, DI Smith wouldn't be asking," Mike said, raising his eyebrows.

Maybe he sensed Bethany wasn't her usual easy-going self today. She silently thanked him for intervening, glad she wouldn't be pushed into saying something she might regret—or get told off for if she got reported.

"Oh my days, no need to get arsey." Julie gave him the side-eye, mouth pursed. "If you must know, it was because of him being a dick, always out with Evan—that's his brother who lives at The Grubby, in case you were wondering. I *knew* Keith would keep going there, saying he was visiting Evan when really he'd be in the pub, downing pints. Before Evan moved there, Keith was always at home, reading his books while I watched a bit of telly. Not anymore. To be honest, when he comes back—today, tomorrow, whenever—I'm telling him if he doesn't shape up, he can bloody well ship out."

He's already shipped out, love, on the cruise to Heaven... Composed enough to continue, Bethany said, "When we arrived, you said about Keith being in trouble. Is that usual for him?" She'd quickly scanned notes on the book clubbers yesterday, and none of them had previous, so Keith being in *that* kind of trouble didn't make sense, unless he was the clever type who'd never got caught.

Julie fiddled with her hair, which didn't even look like it needed a trim, unless she'd lied about the salon trip. "No, but I just thought, you know, brothers together on the razz, geeing each other up, that sort of thing. Keith doesn't handle his drink too well. He's easily led after a few. He's embarrassing. I have to keep him in line at parties."

I bet you do. "Are you aware of anyone who has a grudge against him?"

Julie laughed. "No, except for me from time to time. You know when they just get on your nerves? He does that regularly."

I'd love for Vinny to be here so he could get on my nerves again.

Julie went on, "I really think we're on the verge of splitting, but I keep hanging about because I do care the for the silly bugger."

Or is it for his money, like Evan said? "What did you think when he didn't come home the past two nights?"

"Well, the first one, I told him to stay away, but last night? I just thought he'd decided to give me more space. I was pretty raging, so I don't blame him. Anyway, it shows he's learning. At last."

Is she for real? Learning? Poor bastard. "Did he message you at all during that time?"

"No."

"And is that normal?"

"God, yes. When I say leave me alone, it means exactly that."

I can well imagine. "You didn't message him either then?"

"No. Best I didn't while I've been musing along the lines of ending it. I needed to think properly, to make sure. But I finally decided. One more chance, then we're over. You can't keep hanging around hoping they'll mend their ways, can you? Some men just can't be moulded."

Oh. She's one of those. Picks a bloke and changes them to what she wants them to be. Lovely. I need to get out of here before I snap at her. "Do you have a friend or family member available to sit with you today?"

Julie frowned. "What the hell for? Like I said, I'm going to get my hair cut. Anyway, they'll all be at work. I have the day off. Mind you, next door might be in. And you didn't answer me. What for?"

You didn't give me the ruddy chance. "I'm sorry to have to bring you bad news, but Keith's body was found this morning."

Julie blinked. Laughed. Quietly, unsteadily. Nerves? "Pardon?"

Bethany repeated it. Waited.

The waterworks lasted about three minutes, oddly, no actual tears, just the noises, eyes scrunched up, mouth skewing, then Bethany handed Julie her card. They left her dabbing at mascara that hadn't even run, her action all for show, although why she bothered to do that, Bethany didn't know. From their short conversation, it was clear Julie was self-absorbed and didn't really care about Keith like she'd professed.

Evan was right after all. She wasn't nice underneath that well-put-together veneer.

"She could be saving the tears for later," Mike said as they drove away.

"So why the racket? Why fake-cry for our benefit? Stupid woman." *God, I could do with some sleep.*

"Maybe she thought that was what we expected."

"It wasn't necessary, though, was it? You and I know some people cry, some don't. Some get angry, some get maudlin right off the bat. If she didn't feel like crying, fine, but don't put it on. Underhand behaviour, that is, and shows her character for what it really is."

They didn't speak anymore, Bethany too riled up by Julie's performance, Mike most probably knowing that and leaving her to stew by herself, which was smart. She wouldn't want to snap at him either. He was her best friend now Vinny had gone, and she didn't like barking.

At Shadwell Hill, she pulled over to sign the log at the start of the track, then drove up to the car park, leaving hers where she had before, beside Presley's red one. Suited up, she led them to the tent, the summer sun heating it up so the air inside had the taint of death to it, that first scent of a dead body breaking down internally. It would get worse as the day wore on. She shivered, despite the warmth, and said hello to everyone.

"Strangulation again," Presley said, getting down to it straight away. "Same killer. I found no pattern to the tacks while studying them last night—the ones on Susan's body, obviously—and these ones also look random." He waved vaguely at Keith. "What do you think about the forehead ticks?"

"Possibly exactly what they are, him ticking off who he's killed," Bethany said.

Isabelle frowned. "I don't get the random toe chop. It was bugging me in bed when I was supposed to be going to sleep."

"No idea here either," Mike said. "Maybe we're wrong about ticking people off and—"

"They're people who've ticked *him* off?" Presley suggested.

"That's a good one, too," Mike said, "but I was going to say, maybe they're just literally something to do with tic-tac-toe and nothing more. We could be looking into this more than necessary."

"The killer may well have done this subconsciously," Isabelle said. "Let's get inside a warped head for a minute. The noughts and crosses could just be a grid to show us he intends to kill nine. He knows the American name for it and utilised that to do the tick, tacks, and toe, but deep in his mind, the ticks could well be either reason we've come up with today, the tacks could possibly be him taking a 'different tack' than he has before with these people, and the toe—they didn't toe the line?" She shrugged. "We could speculate for hours and still not come up with the correct answer. That's something we'll hopefully find out when they're caught."

"The thing is," Bethany said, "we have to think of these things in case they're clues. If we unravel the why, we're more likely to find the who."

"At the same time, you don't want to be chasing rainbows." Isabelle sighed. "The lack of CCTV footage doesn't help with Susan, and seeing as there aren't any cameras out this way, as we learnt on previous cases involving this bloody hill, you'll get minimal sightings just before the cameras cut off, and they'll be grainy anyway."

"Aren't we all just a bundle of positivity today," Bethany grumbled.

"Better to face facts than dream for the impossible," Presley said.

Bethany stared around at everyone. "Do we all need to get together for a mad drinking session when this is all over or what? It's like we're in sore need of letting our hair down."

"Not for me," Presley said. "You know I don't mix business with pleasure."

"I'm all for it." Isabelle perked up. "We could get our teams together and bombard somewhere. It'd be a right laugh. God knows we need one."

"Okay, that's settled then. We'll arrange the date once this is wrapped up."

A phone chimed.

"That's mine." Bethany took it out. "A message from Fran, asking me to ring her. Won't be a sec."

She left the tent, tugging down her hood, thankful for the fresh air outside. Even though her phone worked with gloves, she took them off and put them in her pocket, then swiped her screen and accessed Fran's name in her contact list.

"Hi, Fran, it's me."

"I just wanted to touch base. Too much to type in a message."

"Okay, we're back at Keith's scene now. That Julie was a weird one."

"How do you mean?"

"She pretended to cry when we told her."

Fran gasped. "What? Who *does* that?"

"I thought the same. I think it pissed me off because my tears for Vinny... Well, you get my drift. Hers? She just made sobbing noises, no tears."

"Strange."

"Anyway, give me what you've got then."

"Okay, CCTV on the roads that lead to the hill— bugger all we can work with, but we knew that was going to happen. I've been on Keith's social media—he had Facebook and Instagram. Pretty sparse, although Julie loves putting up selfies and tagging him. Perhaps telling is there are a lot with her and Keith together when they first started going out, but lately, she's by herself a lot."

"That makes sense after what she said to us. Go on."

"She's into those cryptic memes that hint at things but don't actually say it. The sort where you'd understand what they meant if you were in the know regarding her life. They could indicate she planned to end their relationship, all that 'be by yourself to know yourself' gumph."

"Definitely right. She told us she was going to give him one more chance then finish with him. What about other people?"

"The only friend they have in common online is Evan. She has a few pals who do the usual 'Are you all right, hun?' when the vague-booking goes on. Keith's a member of a group—Book on the Positive Side. He doesn't post in there so must have just used it for recommendations. I'm guessing here. From the digging Leona did by asking more questions when she phoned the book clubbers to warn them to be vigilant, none of them are friends outside the library, not counting Claire Billing and Wendy and Rhiannon Tynen. As we know, they're family."

Bethany digested everything for a moment then came to the conclusion that basically, there were no bloody leads. Now why wasn't she surprised? "So the deaths aren't connected because of friendship, but they could be from association. I hope to God we don't find one of the others dead. It'd definitely be about the library then, surely."

"Hmm. Well, we'll keep poking about on our end and see if we can find anything. Once the CCTV showed nothing, I sent Glen and Talitia to Keith's street to start questioning neighbours."

"Brilliant, that saves me and Mike doing it. We were there, obviously, to see Julie, but needed to pop back here in case Presley had found something we could work with. I'd planned to do house-to-house after this. Anyway, Presley didn't find anything new. Same cause of death as Susan."

"I wonder if strangulation was chosen so they could look in their eyes while they were doing it— or to make sure the victims saw their killer. Scrap that, of course they saw them. They'd have—"

"Two seconds, Fran. I think my name's just been called. Stay on the line." Bethany rushed into the tent. *Shit, no gloves on…*

"Gun pressed to the temple and his back," Mike said. "Plus, Keith had a knock to the opposite side of his head. There's just a slight lump and faint bruising."

"Okay. Presley, did you measure that indent on Susan yet?" Bethany asked.

"I did, and I compared it to all the known guns, and none of them match. I sent you an email earlier. There's a picture of the indent."

Crap, she should have checked. "So they're using a gun we haven't seen before." She stared at the ground, thinking. "Then it would have to be illegal, no trace. Bugger." She darted outside again. "Did you get all that?" she asked Fran.

"Yep. Can you send me that image? We can get to work on foreign guns and do comparisons. At least we'd get some idea of where it came from, and that might help us."

"I'll do that now. We'll be back soon anyway. I need to write on the whiteboard so we're all on the same page. Talk later." She ended the call and forwarded Presley's email to Fran—he hadn't written anything on it the team shouldn't see, just: *No matches. Attached is a photo of the indent.* Plain and simple, as usual.

In the tent yet again, gloves on this time, she was treated to the sight of Presley showing her where the gun had marked Keith. She had a chat with everyone—more speculation—then decided it was time to head off. The air was getting stifling and even more pungent, and flies buzzed around the tick on Keith's forehead, one crawling around the belly-button toe.

It was too much.

"Before you go," Isabelle said, "after you left earlier, I sent Keith's phone in to digi. Hopefully, there'll be something found on there."

"Thanks. We're away now. I have a feeling we'll see you soon." Bethany walked out, eager to get her suit off. She stuffed it in the box beside the SOCO van, adding the booties and gloves.

In the car, she handed Mike her packet of wet wipes after she'd pulled a few out. God, for some reason, it was as if death had got deep into her skin. A quick wash of sorts had her feeling better, then they were on their way back to the station.

She'd fill in the whiteboard, do some paperwork, and have a meeting with her team once Glen and Talitia got back from doing door-to-door. Oh, and somewhere in there, she'd have some lunch. That Coco Pop bar hadn't done a proper job, and her stomach was rumbling.

Noisy git.

CHAPTER ELEVEN

"How long will she stay asleep for?" Erica poured a coffee from the freshly brewed carafe.

The kitchen smelt heavenly, rich with the scent of Brazil's finest. While Lenny took his time over answering her—too busy gawping at someone's tits on his phone, she'd bet—she thought about this afternoon. She had a meeting later with a client who wanted her husband killed tonight, and Erica needed the caffeine to get her through it. There'd be the usual conversation, mainly one-sided on the customer's part, which would involve a lot of simpering and Erica wanting to give the wife a pass to Heaven, too, free of charge.

"About six hours." Lenny finally pulled his attention away from his screen. He watched far too many sexy ladies on there.

If she loved him, it would hurt.

"Pour me one, will you?" he said.

That river was calling his name pretty loudly right this minute, but she stifled the urge to deck him, strangle him, then dump him in it. Instead, she grabbed a fresh cup out of the cupboard. Most times, it was sensible to do the right thing.

Most times.

"Six hours? That is not enough," she barked. "She needs to be asleep until the guests have gone." She sorted his cuppa. "We need to get that room cleaned and the furniture back in straight after we let her go, then if she tells the police what she saw and they come round, there will just be a normal bedroom. I do not need to tell you how much this can fuck everything up. We have a good deal here. We have people who know what I do and pass business my way—no one tells on us because they are too frightened to. It has taken me years to get to this point. We do not need authorities sniffing around. I do not have to tell

138

you how angry I will be if I have to move countries again. I have already left Russia."

"Stop getting your fucking knickers in a twist, will you?" Lenny took the cup from her without saying thank you.

The sound of gushing water cruising over rocks filled her head. The splash of his body hitting the surface. "I will twist your neck, not my knickers, if you continue to speak to me like that. I have told you before about one boyfriend and what I have done to him. You will be next."

"Yeah, yeah. You love me too much to do that."

She imagined staving his head in with a stone from the riverbank and smiled.

"See?" he said. "You can't stay arsey at me for long."

She let him think he was right. "Jambrea will need more gear when she wakes. Enough to keep her out of it until I have removed her from the house." She'd lied to him. No police would come calling, asking about illegal immigrants, because Jambrea wouldn't be around to tell them.

"I'll deal with her," Lenny said.

"No, we clean up our own messes. She is my mess; she came here to see me, not you."

"Fair enough." Lenny sniffed. "Saves me the hassle. It's just that I had the idea of taking her with the guests, seeing if she could be put to good use elsewhere. She wouldn't be able to ring the coppers then, locked up in someone's basement as a sex slave or whatever, and I might make some money off the sale of her. We could up the holiday to all-inclusive then."

Him and this bloody holiday. "I will convince her to move away, keep her mouth shut." Erica hadn't found a man who thought along similar lines as her—but him saying he'd get rid of Jambrea… Hmm. Maybe she'd keep Lenny. She'd see how things panned out. "I will give her money."

"Eh? How much?"

Or maybe she *would* get rid of him after all. His question suggested she had to run it by him if she wanted to spend her cash. "That is none of your business. What I do with my money is my concern. What time do the guests leave?"

"Eight." He slurped his drink.

The river burbled. Two birds cawed from the surrounding trees, flapping their midnight wings inside her head, then they crashed into each other, creating a murder of crows. She gripped the edge of the worktop. "Then I will take Jambrea out at the same time." *Although the actual taking out will be about twenty minutes later.* She smiled again.

"What's so funny?" Lenny asked.

"Nothing."

"Then why are you grinning?"

"I am going to enjoy killing you, nosy insect."

"You're hilarious."

You will not be thinking that when I am suffocating you.

Zac had spent the last two hours wondering where the hell Jambrea was. This was the longest run she'd ever been on, so unless she'd stopped off to chat to one of her friends, he didn't have a clue. She wouldn't be seen dead these days in the city centre with running clothes on, so shopping was off the table. Besides, her bag was still here, and her purse was in it—he'd looked, had a good nose in it, too. Lots of receipts for makeup and one for perfume. Alien. Well expensive. Easy to see where his money was going, the cheeky cow.

She was messing with his plans by doing this. He had somewhere to be in half an hour, and he needed her asleep from the gear so she wasn't aware he'd left the house. If she didn't come back, he'd have to go out regardless—no way he could put this off. Today was his one chance to get the third person at a specific moment, otherwise it wouldn't be poetic, wouldn't mean so much.

He paced the living room, looking out of the window every now and then, anxiety biting chunks out of his gut. Shit, when he got home later, he'd have to make out he'd seen a potential new customer—because she'd ask what he'd been up to, no doubt about that. If he could get her to swallow his lies until day nine, that would be brilliant.

Time was up, so he left the house and drove towards the allotment the old duffer used. In fifteen minutes, at one o'clock, after having his lunch in his shitty little deckchair beside his spring onions and slug-bitten lettuces, the bloke would walk down the track along the side, then across a field. Beyond that was the estate he lived on. Zac had to get him before he made it home, and he'd scoped out just the place.

He swerved off the empty main road—the universe was aligning—and onto the field, driving along until he reached a stand of oaks and birches, which were planted far enough apart down the middle to allow his vehicle to glide through.

A stumbling block presented itself in the form of a kid's bike propped against a tree. It had stabilisers on it.

He parked and got out, heart banging away, and approached the bike. Pink and white. Something shuffled, and he spun around. A girl stood there, must be about four years old, blonde hair in a low ponytail. She stared, eyes wide, darting her gaze from him to her bike, lifting a chubby hand to suck her thumb. What the fuck was she doing out here on her own? Was her mother about?

"Where's your mum?"

She didn't answer.

"You need to fuck off," he said, The Voice of Fear a growl. "Go on, piss off out of it." He pointed at her bike. "Get on that and go home. And you didn't see me, right?"

Tears filled her eyes, and she nodded, her bottom lip wobbling. She got on her bike and pedalled off at speed, across the field towards the estate. This was all he fucking well needed, some brat getting him in the shit.

He thought about Keith being horrible to him as a teen, rude, and how he'd felt about it, yet *he'd* just been rude to that girl.

What was wrong with him?

Should he go home? She might tell her mum a nasty man had been mean, and the dad might come here and bugger things up.

No. It has to be here, today.

He ran a few metres to the bushes at the back of the allotment and waited at the corner. Caught his breath. Made sure the kid had gone.

She had.

He peered through the greenery to check if the wanker was coming yet.

He was, the five-foot-nothing fucker, hands in his trouser pockets, whistling some tune or other from the fifties or sixties. Zac didn't listen to it properly, otherwise he'd remember that whistle from before, what it represented, and he didn't like remembering. Not that.

Shit, could he even do this one? Just the idea of touching that man again—and he'd have to—was gross.

"You've got this sorted, no problem," he muttered, using The Voice of Fear again.

The grey-haired twat was halfway down the track now, and, as usual, he pulled his hands from his pockets and brought out a packet of fags. Marlboro, the ones with the really bad smell.

Come here, Zac, and light this for me.

Come here, Zac, and take my cup into the kitchen.

Come here, Zac, and—

143

He pushed the orders out of his head, and the memory of how that cigarette smoke had always chuntered out of the man's mouth every time he spoke. How Zac's eyes had itched from it, and his stomach churned at having to do something for him yet again.

Five years that bastard had lived with them, his dad's mate, supposedly down on his luck.

And for five years, Zac had been his skivvy. His—

Don't.

What sort of 'family friend' *was* he? What sort of parents allowed it and didn't notice what had happened later? Thank God they'd died years ago. Two less crosses to add to his grid.

Concentrate. He's getting closer.

Bert Yawling, I'm coming for you.

As the duffer got to the edge of the track...

Zac sprang out. "Boo!" He smiled then laughed. "Your *face!*"

Bert stared at him, cigarette smouldering on the grass where it had dropped from his fingers, his hand plastered to his chest. His cheeks, ruddy as anything, had those nasty red spider veins Zac remembered so well.

Drink did that.

Come here, Zac, and pour me a whiskey.

"What the bloody hell are you playing at?" Bert bent to retrieve his fag, groaning at the audible crack from his back or knees. He toked until his cheeks sucked in. Inhaled. Blew the smoke in Zac's direction.

Adding fuel to the fire.

Zac glanced past Bert. The hedges also went down the side of the allotment, tall, so unless some nosy parker was of a mind to peer over, no one would see them standing here. Then he checked behind him. The estate was too far away for anyone looking out of a window to be able to make out who they were. Who Zac was.

He had to get a move on because of that kid.

"Fancy a bevvy?" he asked.

Bert's eyes lit up, then they narrowed. "Now why would you want to buy me a drink? I haven't seen you for nigh on fifteen years."

But I've seen you. I've been watching. Keeping tabs.

"Got to thinking, didn't I." Zac shrugged. "People from your childhood shape you, make you who you are as an adult. Thought we could talk about a few things."

"What sort of things?" Bert took another drag, eyeing him shiftily.

"That's what the chat's for. Come on, my car's over here." Zac strolled away and hoped the lure of alcohol would sway Bert. If it didn't, he'd just punch the old bastard in the face and get him into the trees that way.

Contingency plan.

He giggled.

"Wait up!" Bert called.

Got you.

Zac slowed and turned, walking backwards. "Get a move on. The Grubby's got a happy hour between one and two. We don't want to miss out."

Bert upped his pace, flicking his ciggie to the side. It landed in the lush grass, smoke coiling upwards between the blades, the orange burn of the ember peeking through then winking out. "Hang on. I'm not as young as I used to be. My hips can't take it."

Fuck your hips. "The car's just here, look."

Zac spun to jog forward and open the boot ready. Bert was still trundling along, a few feet from the tree line. Zac unzipped the kill bag and took out the black rag he'd used for the other two. There was something satisfying about stuffing the same one in their mouths. They were all connected in another way then, not just to him, but to each other. He held it in his fist, screwed up so Bert wouldn't see it.

Finally, the ancient fart ambled into the trees, aiming for the passenger side. Zac whipped the gun from the bag and stuffed it in the waistband of his jeans. He came out from behind the car, smiling, like everything was hunky-fucking-dory, when it wasn't, it really wasn't.

Come here, Zac, and pull off my shoes.

No. No.

Come here, Bert, and have this rag shoved down your throat.

Bert reached out to open the door. Zac walked behind him, slapped his hand onto Bert's forehead, drew him backwards against his chest, and

146

rammed the rag into his mouth. Was that his *teeth* clacking there? The old git had *dentures*?

Zac laughed while Bert mumbled something and brought his hands up to grip Zac's hand. No. Not allowed. Zac let go and clutched Bert's wrist, lowering his arm then pinning it behind Bert's back. He took the gun out and dug it into the crepe-like temple. Gave it a good poke until Bert cried out around the rag.

"Now then, you're going to do what *I* say for a change," Zac snarled, The Voice of Fear menacing. "Move."

He kneed him in the arse, guiding him to the boot. There, still holding his wrist, he pushed the back of Bert's head with the gun hand until his brow rested beside the kill bag. Bert kicked out with one leg, catching Zac's shin.

"You can't hurt me anymore," Zac jabbed the gun into his waistband again then reached into the bag for the soft rope.

Bert had a long-sleeved cotton shirt on, so that solved the problem of skin chafe. Zac didn't want the police to know he had to tie them up. Better that they thought fear ensured his victims complied. He secured Bert's wrists then yanked him upright by the hair, twisting him round so the backs of Bert's thighs pressed onto the boot rim.

"How does it feel to be the one who isn't in charge?" Zac asked. "The one who can't say no? The one who has to do as he's told whether he wants to or not? That's how you made me feel— trapped, worthless—and then, later on down the

147

line of my bloody crap life, you said: *Come here, Zac, and suck my toe.*"

Bert's eyes widened, and he snorted while breathing, snot flying out. Saliva dribbled from the corners of his mouth and down his chin, the filthy nonce cretin.

"And while I was doing that, with you telling me if I didn't, there'd be trouble, you followed it up with: *You tick all my boxes, son. All my boxes.* Do you have any idea what that's done to my fucking head?" He gripped Bert's throat, anger taking over, steering him off the planned path and onto a different road.

Stop. Stop. Take a breath.

He sucked in a lungful of air, staring to the side so he didn't have to see the nasty face of the man who'd set all these balls rolling. The one who'd opened Zac's eyes to people who were mean to him, using him, and look what had happened. Everyone who had ever dogged him off, made him feel uncomfortable, or useless, or unworthy...they were all going to cop it because of Bert.

"Why did you put those tacks on my belly?" Zac asked, calmer, his own voice back. "Why did you pull them out and lick the blood? What kind of sick pervert *are* you? I was a kid when you started the weird shit. You were middle-aged and knew better, yet you still did it all. Do you see what you've created? Do you?"

Bert nodded frantically, said what sounded like *Sorry!*, but the rag distorted it.

Zac shook his head. "But not half as sorry as I am that it's come to this. And d'you know what set me off? Seeing some littluns playing that fucking game. That grid. The one you used to draw in your notepad. You win, I suck not just your toe..." *Christ Almighty, this one's difficult. So bloody difficult.* "I win, I do the same again. Tic-tac-unfair-toe. You ruined me."

A tear ran down Bert's cheek.

"Yeah, you're upset now, when you know what's coming next. You weren't upset at the time, though, were you? Only now when it matters to you. Weren't bothered when you whistled after getting your end away, the kind of whistle that says you're happy, you got what you wanted." Rage built. "Get on the ground."

He threw him down, and Bert stumbled in the direction of the field, and it was clear his instinct was to get home, to safety, and then everything would be all right.

Except it wouldn't be. Not for him.

Zac swiped up his kill bag and ran over to him, punching the back of his head. The bastard went down on his knees, and the rag and dentures shot out. Bert inhaled, ready to scream, so Zac elbowed him in the temple, knocking him onto his side. He kicked him in the gums, Bert groaning, then grabbed the rag and stuffed it back in his gaping, despicable gob. He rolled him onto his back and straddled him, placing the bag next to them.

"Now," he said, "on this lovely summer afternoon, I'm going to kill you, fifteen years to the day when you first put your disgusting, nasty prick where it shouldn't go. I hope you end up in Hell."

Afterwards, when he'd finished his usual ritual, plus an extra something, he drew a chalk grid on a wide tree trunk, filling the top row with crosses.

Job complete.

He walked to his car.

And whistled.

CHAPTER TWELVE

"**Y**ou are bloody *kidding* me!" Bethany stared at her desk monitor. It wasn't on, and with the three o'clock sun coming in through the window behind her, her reflected shape on the screen was a silhouette. She pressed the phone closer to her ear and wished she hadn't heard what she had. It was going to be one of *those* days.

"Not kidding, sorry. Wish I was," Rob said.

Going by the drumming sound, she imagined him tapping his fingers on the front desk, and he was probably wondering whether to crack a joke or behave himself.

"Right," she said. "Why the change of time? They've been killed at night before. Why…? Don't answer me. Talking to myself. Okay, we'll go there now." She put the phone in the cradle.

Isabelle's going to lose her shit. She hasn't finished at Keith's scene yet.

Bethany strode out of her office, glad she'd at least done all her to-do list and eaten some lunch. The chat with her team had basically been going over everything and, like in the tent earlier, waffling a lot of supposition and not enough fact.

She barged into the interview room. "We've got another one."

"I knew it," Leona said. "I had a bet going with Fran that this'd be a serial. That'll be you making me coffee all day tomorrow, my friend."

"Bugger." Fran feigned being distraught.

Bethany shouldn't laugh about bets like that, but she did, and some of today's tension seeped away. If she could get to bed early tonight, she'd catch up on the lost hours and be a kinder bunny tomorrow.

"He was found by some children, unfortunately. They'd gone to the copse behind an allotment to play 'dens'." Bethany gave them the allotment address. "Okay, Fran, Leona, get on with digging—and I don't mean for vegetables."

Groans went round.

"You didn't find that amusing? Shame. The victim is a Bert Yawling, sixty-three. Lives on Broadland Road, number ten. Glen, Talitia, door-to-door in Broadland, please—sorry, I know you've only just got back from doing Keith's street. I want to know what this man was like, where he went, his patterns, the lot. Did he have a routine? Is that why someone knew where he'd be today, because, quite frankly, to casually bump into a man in a small copse behind a sodding allotment is a bit of a stretch for me—unless these murders are random and the killer just happened to be there, as did Bert. Doubtful. Check if this fella is a member of the library." She directed that at Fran and Leona. "Ring the book clubbers and ask them if they know him—don't let on why you're asking, for Pete's sake, although they'll probably catch on." She clapped. "Right, let's get to it."

"Before you go, you need to know something." Leona grimaced.

"What?"

"Peter Uxbridge has let the cat out of the bag. He's even spoken to Susan's neighbours. Plus..."

"Show me, quickly."

BODIES FOUND IN CAR PARKS—COINCIDENCE?

PETER UXBRIDGE – REGIONAL CRIME

The body of Susan Burrow was discovered yesterday morning by her co-worker, Michele Oberlander. Susan ran the library and had been alone the previous night after a book club meeting. She hadn't had time to lock the doors—someone had used a gun against her temple then murdered her in the car park.

Our source with Shadwell police had this to say:

"Susan was a well-liked individual who wouldn't hurt anyone, so her murder is particularly baffling. We're unsure as to why she was murdered, but rest assured, we'll find the killer."

Neighbours of Susan were shocked and upset, one of them saying, "I can't believe she's gone. She did so much for this community, running the library, always there if you needed a cup of sugar or whatever. There's no one I can ask for that sort of thing now. I'm so gutted."

A second body was found this morning. Roslynn Ernst, a dog walker, found it and was too distraught for comment. The deceased, Keith Crow, was a member of the book club at the library and had been at the meeting with Susan Burrow the night before his death.

Our informant said, "We're looking into this as related. Both people had ties to the library. What is disturbing us is the manner the bodies were treated. The second biggest toes have been chopped off and placed in belly buttons. The use of drawing pins pressed into the stomachs is particularly strange, as is a carving of a tick on each forehead. The skin has been removed from the scene by the perpetrator. Close to the bodies were grids for noughts and crosses, leading us to believe the killer sees this as a game. We also believe car parks are significant, given that both victims were found in one. If you know of anyone who has been acting oddly recently, call us."

Well, whatever the killer is up to, it's not good. Stay safe, folks!

"I didn't even think about the bloody car parks being a clue," Bethany said. "Shit." The idea of Uxbridge pointing that fact out, via whoever the little bastard was who kept leaking information, had her blood boiling. She wanted to kick herself for missing that, but then again... "But he's wrong. Bert Yawling is in a copse, so stick that up your arse, Peter." She let out a breath. "Saying the deaths are related—we're just guessing, it isn't fact. And as for giving out so much detail this time... Who from this station is talking to Uxbridge?"

Everyone else shrugged.

"When I find them..." She gritted her teeth. "Enough of worrying about him—and I'm sorry if you get a load of calls from the public while we're out. That'll slow you down. I'm going before I have a shit fit."

"Um, can you wait a sec?" Leona asked. "There's something else. A couple of things actually."

Lord have bloody mercy and give me the will not to explode. "Yes?"

"Firstly, none of the foreign guns I've checked have the same look as the indent image. I've asked a PC to go over them again, just in case my eyes were glazing. The second thing is, we've had a report back from digi. The library computer."

"And?"

"Susan used it after ten o'clock, once everyone had gone home. She removed fines from a few people's accounts." Leona shrugged. "Why would she do that? Okay, maybe she realised those fines were a mistake, fair enough, but to do them at that time?"

Bethany could relate. "What if she did it before she forgot? You know how it is. You think of something and have to do it right away, otherwise it won't get done until you remember again. Did you get a list of names for the ones that had been removed?"

Leona nodded. "There's seven of them."

"Then add that to your lovely long list of things to do. Ring them. See how well they knew Susan, plus if they know Keith and now Bert."

She waited for Mike to get up, said goodbye, then they walked out of the station into lovely sunshine.

Must remember to put a washload on before bed so I can hang it out in the morning.

She snapped out of the mundane and drove them to the scene, still fuming about the news article but telling herself to put it out of her head. Uxbridge would get a kick out of riling her, so if she bumped into him on her travels, she'd make out he hadn't naffed her off. Although that might change if the rest of the day got her goat.

She went down a track alongside an allotment. A high hedge prevented her from seeing if anyone was inside, and once they'd viewed the body, that would be their second port of call unless Fran or Leona got hold of her with the next of kin.

A housing estate stood in the distance on the other side of a field, and she took a right at the end of the track, the small copse a couple of hundred metres ahead. A SOCO van had been parked in front of it, and she could just make out white-suited officers between the trees and a tent being erected.

She stopped behind the van, and they togged up.

"I was thinking on the way here… This killer doesn't have a specific type," Mike said, drawing the zip up over his belly. "A woman, a man, an old man. They're all different, but somehow, they're connected. If Bert Yawling isn't anything to do with the library, then this is more complicated."

She put gloves on, her outfit complete. "I'm determined to catch whoever it is. What they're doing is sick, and they need to be bloody stopped and thrown into prison. There ought to be something we can charge Uxbridge with so he can have a stint inside an' all. And that bloody copper doing the leaking." *Don't think about them. Concentrate on the job.* "You ready?"

"Yep. And I agree, but Uxbridge is only writing what he's been told. It's the leaker I'm more bothered about. What gets me is how they talk as if it's me or you, all this 'looking into this as related' business. We thought it might be, but if Bert isn't anything to do with the library, whoever is giving out information will have to backtrack when they next speak to Uxbridge."

"Fuck them for now," Bethany said. "We need to get on."

They entered the copse, and a few paces in, stopped to sign the log held out by an officer she didn't know. Maybe they were new, maybe they'd been around for ages and she just hadn't encountered them before. They continued on, dipping beneath the police tape strung up between two thin tree trunks, heading towards Isabelle, who stood watching the tarpaulin being pulled forward over the front of the tent frame.

"Didn't expect to see you so soon," Isabelle said, "at least not until the early hours of tomorrow morning, yet here we are, a daytime kill. I've had a quick look. Same shit, new body, although there's a little surprise for you this time."

"Oh God, what?" Bethany's stomach muscles clenched, squeezing the sandwich and Frazzles she'd scoffed earlier.

"You'll just have to see, won't you. It isn't a surprise if I tell you what it is." Isabelle smiled. "Come on, let's go in—the tent's sorted."

Thankfully, it was cooler inside than Keith's, what with the shade from the trees. A halogen light had been placed in the corner, and a SOCO switched it on, bathing everything in its unique brightness. Bethany ignored the body while the photographer got to work. She was happy to chat shit with Isabelle and Mike: The state of Chief Kribbs' new haircut—did he think he was twenty or what? (That came from Isabelle.) The fact that the station vending machine now had Starbars in it, and wasn't that just the bloody business, except they sold out quickly, and that was well annoying. And the idea of clubbing together to collect enough money to give to Presley so he could get an extra-special urn to put his cat's ashes in.

Bethany's eyes stung. "That's a really nice thought."

"Pack it in, or you'll set me off," Isabelle said. "Ah, the photos are done. We've been saved from running down the tearful road."

They stepped around SOCOs who were on hands and knees.

"There isn't a grid on the ground this time, but there *is* one on that tree trunk there. Three crosses." Isabelle stood beside the body and pointed. "But look at that."

Bethany didn't.

Mike must have. "Oh, ouch! What the sodding hell?"

Get it over with. See what they're seeing.

Bethany gave the body her attention. Bert was naked. The tick was in place. The tacks. The toe. And... "Oh. Oh God..." She swallowed hard.

A tack had been pressed into the hole at the end of Bert's penis.

"What is this saying?" she said. "Is it suggesting Bert's private parts should be plugged up? Do we have a sex abuse case here?"

159

"Like how cutting a dick off implies the same?" Mike asked.

"Yes. But what's that got to do with Susan and Keith?" She frowned. "Don't tell me they were all secretly involved in some perverted sex ring." She rubbed her forehead with the back of her gloved hand.

"It's something we'd have to consider, obviously." Mike coughed. "Such a small thing, that tack being placed there, but it says so much and changes the way we view this case. The other two weren't naked, apart from their torsos so the tacks and toes could be displayed, so Bert here, being fully naked—and where are his clothes?—we assume he's the one who dished out the abuse."

"Or if not the abuse, the actual sex, consented," Isabelle said. "Maybe he put his willy where he shouldn't. You know, had an affair, and someone found out, thought it was disgusting, and did this."

"That would work if there weren't other victims," Bethany said. "I don't know, this is all so bloody weird. Mike, we should go to the allotment, see if anyone's there. We'll nip back after and see if Presley's arrived, but if he hasn't, we'll visit the next of kin if we even know it by that point. Presley will just have to send me a message if he finds something else different to the other two."

She waved at Isabelle and walked out, Mike beside her. She drove them down the track to the front of the allotment, entering between open double gates with diamond-wire fencing inside black iron frames. Like that was going to keep people out. Anyone with cutters and the need for a bit of veg to go with their chicken and mushroom pie could get inside. That or climb over. A small car park, enough for around four vehicles, was ahead, a metal shed and a water tap at the end of it, so she stopped there and got her bearings.

To the right, a lengthy stretch of vegetable patches went as far back as the rear hedges, each individual garden around fifteen metres square. Beyond the shed to the left were the same patches, some with bamboo sticks like tepee frames, greenery growing up them, others without any at all, veg leaves sprouting from the well-tended ground instead. A man worked on one side in the distance, a second bloke on the other, closer to them, maybe five patches up. He glanced their way, straightened from his bent-over position, and did a bit more planting—of his hands on his hips.

"We'll talk to him first," she said.

They approached, Bethany keenly aware they still had protective clothing on, and that it would tip him off to something being seriously wrong. He stared at them, wide-eyed, his grey bushy eyebrows forming the shape of a bird in flight, how kids drew them, or an open book viewed from the bottom.

"Hello, sir. DI Bethany Smith and DS Mike Wilkins." She showed him her ID.

He leant forward to peer at it, squinting, then took a pair of glasses out of his short-sleeved shirt pocket. With them perched on his nose, he must have had a better view, for his eyebrows sprang apart, forming high arches. "Well now. What's going on here then?"

"Isn't that our line?" Mike chuckled.

The man laughed. Thrust a hand out. "It's a bit dirty, so you don't have to shake. Dave Quantock."

"Best we don't." Mike held up his hands. "Gloves."

Mr Quantock nodded. "Sensible. Something going on then, is it?" He glanced from Mike to Bethany.

"Unfortunately, yes," she said. "Do you know a Bert Yawling?"

"Hmm, him." Mr Quantock sniffed. Disdain or hay fever? "What's he done? Fiddled with a kiddie? I always knew he was one of them."

Bethany's heart pattered faster. "What makes you say that?"

"Always eyeing the children—we live on the same street. Council-owned bungalows down one side, houses on the other. He comes out into his front garden, leans on his gate, and watches them playing out. Not the girls with their skipping ropes, but the lads having a kickabout."

"Could it be that he's lonely?" Bethany asked.

"Not likely." Mr Quantock snorted. "Not with that teenage lad going in there of a nighttime—the most recent one in a long line of them over the years."

Dread seeped into Bethany. *Shit.* "Do you know the teenager?"

"Yes, young Thomas Collins from number twenty-three. My Yvonne got worried and rang that children's helpline, but nothing was done. All that happened was Thomas said he was going in there to read to him because Bert's eyesight's going. A tall story, pardon the pun. His mother accepted her son's reason."

"How old is Thomas?"

"Fifteen. He comes out of Bert's with gifts, you know. Those trainers in a box, Nike, or a rucksack, things like that."

She caught on to the mention of reading. "Do you know if Bert was a member of the library?"

"I don't, no. Was?" Mr Quantock cocked his head. "There are no flies on me."

Clearly. "Yes, was. Mr Yawling is dead. Murdered."

"That's strange. Are you sure you have the right person? He was here a little while ago."

"Oh? How long was he here for?"

"His usual hour. Unfortunately, his patch is that one, right next to mine, so I had to endure his drivel. He left about oneish."

"What was he wearing?"

"A light-blue, long-sleeved shirt, black trousers, which I thought was a bit silly, what with us having such hot weather. The trousers, I mean. Shorts would be better." He pointed to his own. "And white trainers."

"Thank you."

"Did they kill him at home?" His face scrunched in alarm. "My wife, she's at our bungalow. I should go."

"No, he was found in the copse at the back of here," she said and indicated that way. "We have officers in your street, so please don't panic. Did you hear anything going on when Bert left? People talking on the other side of this hedge here, perhaps?" She gestured to it.

"No, when he leaves, I get my deckchair out and stick my radio on for a while, have a nice sunbathe. I might have fallen asleep." He blushed.

After more chit-chat with Mr Quantock, and talking to the other fella, discovering nothing from him as he hadn't heard anything untoward, didn't know Bert, didn't even acknowledge him if they were at the allotment at the same time, Bethany drove them back to the copse.

They put on fresh booties, and Presley gave the same cause of death and estimated it to have happened after one o'clock but obviously before three-fifteen when the kids had found him after school, where they usually played until four. Those kids were at home now, being spoken to by uniforms.

A gun had been pressed to Bert's temple and back. Where his clothes and shoes were was anyone's guess, but she now knew if the killer had taken them and they managed to track him or her down, maybe get to search their house, she'd be looking for the blue shirt, black trousers, and white trainers of a possible paedophile.

CHAPTER THIRTEEN

Erica's eyes glazed over behind her fake bottle-bottom spectacles. Her black wig itched her head. Her client hadn't stopped talking since they'd sat in the corner of The Grubby with lattes and a complimentary free biscuit inside a packet that'd need a chainsaw to get it open if she hadn't used her teeth. This job had been a long time in the planning. They always were. Money had to be saved by the client, cash, in dribs and drabs to save arousing suspicion, and the intervening months between the first point of contact to now was to ensure the customer was certain they still wanted Erica to work for them.

While she routinely requested info to see if a person's murder was justified, she'd found out early on in this convo that the man who needed killing was a despicable piglet, so any extra wordage from this woman was unnecessary. However, Monica Stellar clearly thought otherwise. Erica had already learnt Mr Stellar had wandering hands, stayed out all night with no explanation, and visited a specific sex worker.

Monica had hired someone to follow him and take pictures.

She thrust them down on the table. They splayed in a fan, and Erica whipped them up so other pub-goers nearby didn't cop an eyeful. And if Monica didn't keep her bloody voice down, she'd be joining Lenny in the river.

"And to top it all off, he hits me," Monica said. "There are pictures of the bruises as well. Never my face. He's too clever for that."

Erica browsed them. Yes, a despicable piglet. She looked up at Monica and said softly, "Do you have a trace of paying the private detective? A paper trail?"

"No." Monica shook her head. "I've been stealing money for years out of the till, from the first time he punched me. I paid the detective two-fifty a time over several months."

Mr Stellar owned a lucrative mini-mart. His finances would be scrutinised afterwards. Depending on how much money Monica had stolen, that finance check could either be classed as normal or highly irregular.

"The same for your payment." Monica patted her large, avocado-coloured handbag that disturbingly had the same texture as one as well, all knobbly. "It's in here. Well, half of it, like you said."

"Good. Keep it there until we get to the toilet in a bit." Erica glared at her. "And talk quietly. People will hear you. Do you want to go to prison?"

That did the trick. Monica snapped her mouth shut.

"What amounts were you taking?" Erica asked, following her own advice by speaking low.

"Ten pounds here, twenty there. If you do this every day, it mounts up."

"But not for the amount I charge."

"You only want nine thousand."

She did. The massive amounts other people charged for these sorts of gigs were unnecessary. Besides, Erica enjoyed it, so earning too much for a hobby was obscene.

"I also stole goods—cigarettes, alcohol—and sold them at car boot sales. People ask no questions, see." Monica looked proud of herself. "But that isn't your concern. If my bank account and credit cards are checked, it's all normal."

"I will have to trust you on that," Erica said. "You know what will happen to you if you *forget* to pay me the other half, yes?" She made the sound of a neck breaking. "That is what will happen. The last noise you will ever hear. Do you understand what I am saying?"

Monica bobbed her head. "Yes."

"Excellent. About tonight. Did you write it down?"

"I did. The paper with it all on is in with the money. I did what you said and tore the paper off the pad so the words didn't indent on the ones beneath."

"That is satisfactory. You know I do not want this coming back to me, so"—she created the neck-breaking noise again and acted out the accompanying hand movements—"you keep your mouth shut and act upset when police come. Otherwise..."

Monica clapped like a maniac. "I know. I've been practising in front of the mirror."

"This clapping and your excited face. Stop it. Get used to looking sad. Do you have children with this filthy man?"

"No."

"What about his family?"

"He's only got me."

"Do you have life insurance on him?" *This could be a sticky point.*

"Yes."

Shit. Erica sighed. "When was it taken out?"

"I did it six years ago."

"You have been thinking about this for a long time."

"Yes." Monica's face screwed up.

"I can understand you wanting to get paid due to suffering with him. How much is it for?"

"Two million."

"You earnt it."

"I did."

"One month after police come, I want you to drop the rest of the money where we agreed. Do not leave your house before then. Play the grieving widow. It is important. You want his dick chopped off?"

Monica's head would bounce off if she nodded any harder.

Erica finished the last mouthful of coffee. "I have a tool for that. It will be fifty pounds extra for the penis. Add it to the second payment. Now, we must go to the toilet."

With the money swapped into Erica's bag while they'd squashed themselves into a cubicle, they left The Grubby, Monica getting into her car, Erica walking down the street then around the corner to hers. Inside, she checked the correct amount of money was there. It was. Wig and glasses off, she stuffed them in the glove box for later. She used a wet wipe to scrub at the lurid scarlet lipstick and bright-blue eyeshadow. Clean, she resembled herself once more. Taking off her revolting gold-hued silk blouse and switching it for her usual low-necked top, she thought about Jambrea's phone, which Erica had turned off, and took it out of her pocket.

She pulled gloves on, gave it a good wipe with a cloth until it shone, and drove away, tossing the mobile out of the window on the road with the phone box library at the end of it. Parked outside her home, disguise in a carrier bag, she went inside, catching Lenny sprawled on the sofa being just as filthy as Mr Stellar.

"If you tug that too much, it will fall off." She flopped onto her recliner. "Put it away before I chop it as practise for tonight's job."

"You'd better be back in time to collect Jambrea." He stuffed himself away and sat up.

"I will. Be quiet. I need a nap."

She took her phone out of her pocket and browsed her newsfeed on Facebook, reading a few things here and there until her eyes drooped. She closed them, smiling, thinking of what she'd spend the money on.

Zac had checked the house when he'd got back earlier. Still no sign of Jambrea. He'd phoned her— no answer—and sent a text—again, no answer. Her purse was still in her bag, so she'd be back at some point. Maybe her headache *had* been bad after all and she'd blacked out while running. Or her brain had exploded from the gear. He shrugged. Someone would find her eventually. In the meantime, he'd keep ringing and texting her, so it looked like he still cared.

In their bedroom, he placed Bert's forehead tick on the blackboard with Susan's and Keith's, then stuffed it back under the bed. He took the old man's clothes and trainers into the garden and put them in his barbecue, soaking them with petrol. The flames were beautiful when he tossed a match on top, and he stared at them, entranced.

Someone shouting, calling him a selfish wanker for creating smoke while she had her washing out, pulled him out of his daze. He didn't douse the fire, though, instead waiting for the clothes to become unrecognisable. Once they'd cooled, he used a ladle from the kitchen drawer and scooped up all the ash and small bits of material, then switched to the fish slice to take out the plastic trainer soles that had melted. The ash and material went down the loo, the soles in the boot, ready for disposal when he went out tonight to get the fourth person dealt with.

Hard work, these murdering shenanigans.

Bethany sighed. With no next of kin living in the country, and no friends as such, apart from people he chatted to in his local pub, more acquaintances than mates, Bert appeared to have lived a solitary life. After his marriage had broken down, he'd had no fixed abode for a good few years, then he'd been given the bungalow by the council. Leona had sorted getting hold of the Australian police to pass on the news to the son, and Bert's ex-wife had died three years ago down under from pneumonia.

Had they moved so far away because he was a pervert?

His place, which they'd spent a good two hours searching along with one of Isabelle's teams, had thrown up disturbing evidence that Mr Quantock was right: Bert Yawling liked little boys. His computer, an ancient, big-backed effort, the white casing now beige from cigarette smoke—Marlboro packets resided in various rooms—contained images Bethany never wanted to see again in her lifetime.

An interesting fact cropped up: he preferred teens for his sexual pleasure. Perhaps the pictures of the younger lads, all around ten years old, was the point where he groomed them, and by the time they were older, they accepted what he asked them to do—or made them.

One picture had her going cold, heaving, and coming to a massive realisation. It was a closeup of a toe between lips. The toe beside the big one.

"The logical leap here is that a male Bert abused has killed him," she said to Mike. "But that doesn't explain Susan or Keith. That's the bit I'm struggling with. Were they just practise kills?"

"I don't believe so. The grids—he's clearly showing how many he intends murdering. He's filled out three boxes. The toes are incredibly upsetting for the killer, but why put them in navels? If I'd been forced to suck a toe, you can bet I'd cut it off and shove it up the abuser's arse."

She thought about what Glen and Talitia had told her about their door-to-door enquiries in the street. Most residents had expressed concern that Bert was into lads, yet only Yvonne Quantock, with support from her husband, Dave, had done anything about it. The others had said they didn't want to cast aspersions based on guesswork—even though teen lads had been 'reading' to Bert for many years. Thomas Collins' mother, though, stuck to the tale her son had told her about innocent story sessions, but she insisted Thomas no longer went there. She worked evenings, and none of her neighbours had bothered telling her the visits had continued.

"What gets me is where Mrs Collins thought the trainers and clothing came from," Mike said. "Did she really believe Thomas' friends gave them to him, like she was told by him?"

"Kids can be convincing, and we'll find out how well he lies in a minute."

Mrs Collins had agreed to take the evening off work. She usually started at eight, but they were going there for five when Thomas got home from football practice. Alice Jacobs was coming as family liaison to help the process run smoothly. Thomas may have formed an attachment to Bert, despite what had happened between them—if anything even had—and the lad could break down once he knew Bert was dead. Alice was excellent at dealing with those situations.

"We'll get over there now then," Mike said. "And I'm *not* looking forward to this at all."

"Me neither."

They left Bert's, removing their protective clothing outside and handing it to the log PC at the front door. Bethany felt dirty, on her body and in her mind, after being in that home where so many awful things had happened behind closed curtains. They crossed the road, and at Mrs Collins' door, Bethany hauled in a breath. Then knocked.

The door opened, and a woman stood there, her face blotchy from crying. Her blonde hair, striped with the sneaky beginnings of grey at the roots, hung in a limp ponytail, her fringe getting in her eyes. Bethany showed her ID and introduced them.

"He's in the living room," Mrs Collins whispered. "I had to tell him about Bert being dead. He saw the police outside the house and kept going on at me until I caved in."

"How did he take it?" Bethany asked.

"He looked relieved. Oh God..." Mrs Collins' eyes filled, and tears dribbled from each one. "What's been going on? Is it true what was said before, that Bert's a pervert?"

"We have reason to believe your son was abused by him, yes."

"W-what?"

"Hopefully he wasn't. It's just rumours at the moment, so please don't upset yourself." Bethany smiled, and a car engine cutting off had her turning around. "Ah, here's Alice. If it happens to be the truth, she will get you both through this, okay? Is there a Mr Collins?"

"Yes, but we're divorced. He's in Malta for work."

They waited for Alice to join them on the step, and after she and Mrs Collins had become acquainted, an agreement in place that Alice would step in if Thomas became distressed to the point it was detrimental to his mental health, they went inside.

Thomas sat on the sill of the bay window in the lounge at the back of the house. He looked up when they entered, and with their identities established and everyone seated, Alice on the end of the sofa, closest to Thomas, Bethany dived in.

"What's your relationship with Bert Yawling, Thomas?"

The lad shrugged, cheeks turning red. "It's embarrassing."

"Please understand that we're not here to judge, but we need to find out why someone would have wanted to kill him," Bethany said. "Two other people have been killed in the same way, and with Bert's death, our previous link between the first two victims has now changed. Just take your time and tell us what you did while with Bert in the evenings. You mustn't feel ashamed or blame yourself. Bert was an adult, you are a minor. You have nothing to blame yourself *for*, do you understand?"

Thomas shrugged. Nodded. "He...um...when I was a kid, he just wanted me to read to him, from the newspaper, stuff like that, and asked me to go and get stuff for him—his slippers, his fags, make him a coffee. He gave me pocket money for it. Like, a quid here and there. But once I got to fifteen, like, three months ago, he started asking for different things, and he said if I didn't do it, he'd tell everyone I was a...a paedo."

Bethany jolted at that. *What the hell?* "So you did the things he wanted so he didn't do that?"

Thomas nodded. "He said everyone would believe him. And he said he'd buy me things. I didn't reckon he would at first, but after I'd sucked his...his toe, he got me some Nikes."

Bethany swallowed bile. Mike cleared his throat. Mrs Collins whimpered. Alice remained as professional as ever and reached out so Thomas could take her hand if he wanted to. The poor kid grasped it tight, and Bethany's eyes stung.

"What else did you have to do?" She held her breath.

And he told her what she'd been expecting.

Later, after the harrowing tale had been related, Alice remaining in the house to go over it again when Thomas was ready so she could take a proper statement, Bethany walked down the Collins' path, her face soaked with tears. She got in the car and rested her head back, letting it all out. Mike got in once she'd composed herself, and she glanced across at him.

His cheeks were wet, too.

"He was a monster," she whispered.

Mike nodded, drying his cheeks with his palms. "A monster I'm glad is dead."

CHAPTER FOURTEEN

At ten to eight, Erica stood against a red-brick office block, a slanted shadow giving her more coverage. There were four buildings set around a square tarmac courtyard with space at each side to walk down. Three of the blocks were boarded up tight with steel panels, but the one opposite, where the tramps lived, had one window without steel over it, plus a broken front door.

They were surrounded by a field. She'd parked behind the block where a main road, seldom used at this time of the evening, curved to join a housing estate. It was risky killing someone right now, what with evening light still in residence, but this site was abandoned, only used by the homeless to sleep in, or sex workers for somewhere safe to go with their clients. People stood on the corner up by the edge of the estate but were too far away for her to see their features. If she couldn't recognise them, they couldn't recognise her.

Mr Stellar had apparently been coming here every week for months, five to eight on the dot, according to the trusty PI. Stellar waited here for the woman he'd booked for eight, did the business, then went to the pub, probably to drink a whiskey to congratulate himself on a shag well done.

The homeless, four of them, had been given fifty quid each and told to make themselves scarce for a while, three hours to be precise. Erica looked like she was plying a certain trade herself, what with her outfit, so they'd probably thought that was her reason for getting rid of them. She had the wig back on, the glasses, the makeup, gloves, and the dreadful gold blouse. The material clung to the sweat on her back, cold and uncomfortable. She'd opted for leopard-patterned leggings—ease of movement—and the red high heels had already gone into her backpack, switched for a pair of trainers once she'd paid those men to leave the area.

She did some stretches to get limber. Shook out her hands. Flexed her fingers and thumbs.

The growl of a car engine broke the silence. The slam of a door.

Mr Stellar arrived, from around the back of the opposite building. He must have driven here via the main road. She pressed herself to the wall while he paced the courtyard, probably anticipating the act to come. The wait for the sex worker dragged, him glancing at his watch, Erica keeping her attention on him, her ears cocked for the woman's approach. She imagined her walking across the field behind in bare feet so her heels didn't dig into the grass and get ruined.

Eventually, two minutes late, she appeared from where Stellar had come from, and he stopped his back and forth. They entered the broken doorway, and Erica counted the minutes as they crawled by—thirteen—then the woman tottered out and disappeared the way she'd entered.

Erica sped across the courtyard and into the building. He was in the process of raising his trousers and stopped to stare at her, a frown, then a grin transforming his face.

He thought she was a prosser.

She used that to her advantage, sauntering towards him seductively, past the discarded condom he'd tossed away, and smiled, revolted inside. What he did behind closed doors to Monica was despicable. Erica stared at his hands—hands that curled into fists at home and struck his poor wife.

Erica never had been able to abide a wife-beater. For reasons.

"Want some of this?" she asked him, her accent thickening. She gestured to her lithe body, showing him what he could have if he only said yes. "Can you get it up so soon after doing my friend?" She thought of Jambrea—'*So, are you doing him or what?*'—and held back a shudder. She'd have to use the feelings of distaste to power through the deed.

He chuckled, letting his trousers drop back to his ankles, then yanked down his pants, the eager bastard. "I can go all night long, darlin'."

Really. Unlikely without Viagra. "That is good." She stood in front of him, thrusting her chest out, displaying the goods Zac ogled so much. "There are rules. Do not kiss me, do not touch me; I do not allow that. But I will touch you. Do you like auto-erotic asphyxiation?"

"What's that?"

"I will show you. Play with yourself. You will see how good this is."

She had no idea whether it was or wasn't, but this ruse had worked in the past, her targets eager to try something new, more thrilling. Seemed this man was no different.

He did as she'd said, and she clasped him around his neck, glad the gloves stopped her from feeling his skin.

"I will squeeze, you will get off," she said.

While he tugged on himself, his eyes gleaming, she applied pressure, increasing it by increments the more excited he got. She murmured rude things to him, mimicking the women from the videos Lenny watched on his phone, tightening her grip more now, her overlapped thumbs on his Adam's apple. It took a while, her hands cramping slightly, but she held on, ignoring the strange sounds that burbled out of his mouth.

She'd heard it all before.

Tighter. Tighter.

His eyes bulged, his legs giving way, then she did the final clamp, anticipating his body losing strength, bracing herself to hold his weight. Her biceps contracted, and her thigh muscles took up the slack. Spittle dribbled from his mouth, down his chin and onto the side of her glove, and he held on to his sex piece right up until the last moment.

She gave one final squeeze.

Once he was dead, she let him fall. He thumped onto his back, arms out to his sides, legs bare, pants and trousers bunched above his shiny black shoes. She slung the backpack off and placed it on the floor, away from the body. Took the dick cutter out and, again thankful she had gloves on, did what Monica wanted. Blood oozed. She pinched the end of his sausage between finger and thumb and threw it to land beside the condom.

"You are a dirty boy." She stared down at him, stuffed the cutter inside a Ziplock bag, and rammed it into the backpack. It would need bleaching later.

A sound from outside had her turning to face the filth-smeared window, and she held her breath, pulse throbbing in her ears. It came again—footsteps, then the faint babble of voices. More homeless must have arrived. She closed her backpack and put it on, ready to escape the moment she could. First, she needed to see what was going on so cuffed a small circle in the dirt on the pane and looked through.

Her heart stopped for a beat.

What the fuck was *he* doing here?

Zac Ferguson stood with a woman in front of the opposite building. They were arguing, him with a gun to her temple, his other hand at her throat, pushing her back against the wall beside the steel-covered door. She couldn't make out what they were saying, but by his tone, he was angry. Where had he got that gun? Was it for protection when he met clients who wanted to borrow money? She'd told him not to be so stupid and buy one, but he'd clearly ignored her.

A holdall sat beside their feet, and he let go of her neck, reached down, gun pointed at her, and pulled out some rope. He said something, and the woman turned around, pressing her cheek to the wall, palms up. Gun stuffed in his waistband, he tied her wrists behind her back, then took something else from his bag. Wielding his gun again, he spun her round and shoved what appeared to be a black rag in her mouth. Slapped her cheek. Pushed her to the ground. He sat on her, put the gun in his bag, and brought out a long and slim implement. The early evening sunlight glinted off it—metal.

Erica's heartbeat went haywire. She'd been taught never to interfere with another person's work while it was in progress so remained rooted, her sole mission to get away from here without being seen. It didn't matter what he was doing or that the woman was probably about to lose her life.

He leant forward and used whatever it was on her forehead, the woman bucking and muffle-screaming, her heels drumming the tarmac. Did she owe him money—money Erica knew nothing about? Was this his form of a lesson in what happened of you didn't pay your debts? Why was *he* doing it instead of asking Erica?

"Stupid man," she muttered.

The lady went still, and Zac threw his head back and laughed. He continued with the tool, then held up...her skin? He dropped it into a container he'd taken out of his bag, then switched that tool for another, moving down her body to her feet. She watched, fascinated yet horrified at the same time, unable to believe Zac was capable of this. He took her shoe off and snipped at a toe. Did several other things, which had Erica gasping at his audacity, his inventiveness, even though she'd twigged what he was going to do. He sat on his victim's pelvis and strangled her.

Erica smiled. This would do nicely. It fitted in with what *she'd* done. She'd just have to get inventive herself.

He drew something on the ground then calmly packed up his bag and walked off down the side of the building Erica was in. The purring of an engine came her way, and she let out a sigh of relief that she'd parked her car behind one of the other blocks, not where he'd left his.

The five-minute wait seemed like half an hour.

She walked out and to the body. Stared down at it. The woman had gold discs on her stomach and a toe in her belly button. The news article she'd read before her nap earlier... *Zac* was that killer. She wouldn't have believed he had it in him if she hadn't seen it for herself.

She studied the foot where the missing toe had been. The forehead. A tick. And he'd drawn a grid *The Herald* had mentioned. There were four crosses in it, but he'd only killed two people prior to this, according to the paper. Or was there another body somewhere that hadn't been reported yet or even found? This one, she must be the fourth.

Taking her bag off her back, she checked what she had inside it, then, pleased, she returned to the open building and undid the buttons of Mr Stellar's shirt, pushing the fronts aside. She took off his shoe and used her dick cutter to snip off his knobbly toe. It balanced in his navel nicely, seeing as he had a deep innie. Stanley knife in hand, she carved the forehead tick, mindful to do it in the same way, then peeled the skin and flesh out of its mooring. Zac had taken the woman's with him, so Erica would have to do the same for authenticity. For now, she put it in a Ziplock baggie and stuffed it in the pocket on the front of her backpack.

With the female, she pulled up one of the drawing pins. A few more removed, and she took them to Mr Stellar and stuck them in his belly, enough to create a small smiley face. The bodies looked the same now, apart from the tiny holes left in the woman's stomach, but that was just tough shit. He would get the blame for Stellar, and that was all that mattered.

A stone in hand, she used it to add an X to the grid, then a thought struck her, and she grinned. Laughed quietly. Added another X, six in total.

She slung her backpack on the passenger seat of her car and drove towards home, the light of the day dimming, the sky a bruised pink, streaks of dark-peach clouds stretched across it. On a hilltop with the love of her life, the view would have been beautiful, but she wasn't on a hill, and the love of her life had yet to present himself. One day, maybe, she'd watch a sunset, a man's hand in hers, their hearts connected.

She shoved those thoughts out of her head and slowed her speed in her street, watching for people who might see her with the wig and glasses on. A quick reverse onto the drive, and she dragged the disguise off. The van Lenny had borrowed was gone, so he'd removed their guests while she'd been busy at work. She popped the boot, lifting the lid to peer over it at the houses opposite. No one appeared to be interested in her arrival.

Inside, she left the front door open and ran upstairs to the room, finding only Jambrea in there, slumped against the radiator, snoring, her mouth parted. The silly girl shouldn't have come here. Had she suspected Zac of sleeping around because he'd been acting oddly and going out, when in reality he'd been a murdering bastard?

From her bedroom, she grabbed a pen, the one she used to do crosswords when sleep wasn't forthcoming, and wrote Jambrea's full name on the woman's hand—she needed the police to be aware of who she was, a link to Zac.

The journey down the stairs was arduous, Jambrea draped on Erica's back, Erica gipping her wrists, and she managed to stuff her in the boot quickly, checking over the lid rim again to see if any neighbours were being nosy.

Erica headed back to the office blocks, cautious in case the homeless had returned early or, more annoying, prossers were plying their trade there. Even worse, the bodies had been spotted and the place swarmed with the police. Wig and glasses back on, her backpack in place, she got out and listened, ears pricked for talking or movement. She'd been educated on picking up even the slightest sounds.

The area was empty—she checked inside the open building—so she carried Jambrea slung over her shoulder, close to the other woman, and placed her down. Then strangled the life out of her. Thankfully, there was no struggling with Jambrea still out of it from the gear. Erica carved the forehead and popped it in a Ziploc. She cut off the toe and borrowed more drawing pins from Zac's victim.

Satisfied he'd have to take the rap for her two jobs, Erica got back in her car and, like before, took the way home where CCTV wasn't used. Halfway along the quiet main road, she threw the Ziplocs with skin ticks inside them out of the window, where they landed on the grass verge. In the rearview, she watched them slide into the ditch.

On her driveway, yet again taking off the wig and glasses, stashing them in the glove box, she went inside her house. Put the dick cutter in the washing-up bowl and covered it with bleach. Took off the makeup. Stripped out of the hideous clothes and trainers, so glad to be getting rid of the gold blouse. She had a long, hot shower to wash away the night's work then pulled on her pyjamas.

Out in the rear garden, she burnt her kill outfit, including the red heels, the trainers, and gloves in a large metal flower tub. She thought about the evening's events while staring at the flames, going over everything in her mind until she was happy she'd covered all bases *and* her tracks. The only thing that gave her trouble was whether any neighbours had seen her coming and going, but she was sure they hadn't. Still, they all knew what she was like, how dangerous she became when angry, so would keep their mouths shut or risk her starting on them. Hurting. Threatening.

This estate was good for residents keeping secrets.

With the discovery of Jambrea's body, Zac would be in the limelight as her boyfriend, unable to continue with his killing spree for a while—the police might watch him. Maybe they'd realise it was him who'd killed the others. If he got arrested, it would save her the job of taking him out, which had been her plan from the start when he'd asked her to collect the repayments for him. Just not so soon. She'd wanted his business to be larger, more clients, then she'd off him and take over.

Never mind. She could build it up herself.

The slam of the van door filtering from the front of the house to the back jolted her out of her head and into the now. She left her clothes and footwear smouldering and turned to enter the conservatory. Lenny stood at the internal door that led to the kitchen, his smile wide, and he held up a padded envelope that bulged in the middle.

"The Caribbean, here we come," he said.

"Our day is not over." She stepped inside, locked up the conservatory, and joined him in the kitchen. "We need to clean the bedroom and put everything back."

Lenny frowned. "We? I thought you said we dealt with our own messes."

"My mess was also in that bedroom. We share the job, even though you had more guests than me. I want this done, finished."

"What did you do with her?" He moved to the kitchen drawers and slid the envelope inside one of them.

"I took her somewhere. You do not need to know details. She will not be telling anyone what happened here, I guarantee it."

"Are you sure that was wise, letting her go? She could get worried later down the line and open her mouth."

She will not be opening anything ever again. "Do not concern yourself."

They tromped upstairs, Erica hauling a blue plastic box of cleaning products with her, Lenny carrying the Vax. He took the wood down from the window, plugging the nail holes with filler. While it dried, they washed the walls, the skirting boards, the radiator, the door and frame, the handle, then Lenny dabbed white gloss over the filler. She scrubbed the sill; Lenny put the blind back up. She used the Vax to get piss stains off the carpet where those skinny men had wet themselves while asleep. Together they lugged the furniture back in, and once more, her beautiful spare room resembled one from a hotel, the air fresh and clean instead of stale and manky.

Lenny could still buy her that Yankee Candle, though.

It was midnight.

Erica had another shower, and while she was in there, she checked out of the window to make sure the embers had doused. In bed, she closed her eyes but couldn't sleep. She thought about Zac being the killer. Why was he doing this? What did the game grid, the ticks, the tacks, and the toes mean to him? What had those people done to deserve death? Or had he muscled in on her business, offering himself as a killer for hire?

She wanted to ask him, and one day soon she'd do that, letting him know she was aware of what he'd been getting up to. For now, though, she'd keep it to herself, watch and read the news, see if any more victims turned up.

Just biding her time.

CHAPTER FIFTEEN

Bethany was in that state where she didn't know if she was awake or not. A phone rang in the distance, sounding like hers. Then she knew it was a dream because she stood in the cemetery, clutching a bunch of flowers ready to place them on Vinny's grave. It was cold, winter, the grass frost-rimed, speckles of it glinting on the gravestone in the light of a butter-yellow moon which had an angry face. And that didn't make sense, the cold. Wasn't it summer?

She reached into her pocket to take out her mobile, but it wasn't in there. Shrugging, she bent over to lay the flowers, and a hand suddenly pushed out of the earth, fingers and thumb claw-like, reaching for her. She screamed and stumbled backwards, and her fall had her eyes widening as the wind got knocked out of her.

She landed and stared at her bedroom ceiling, out of breath, chest tight, her heart thrumming so hard it was painful.

Her phone rang on. Insistent. *Answer me, answer me, answer me.*

"Fuck!" She scrabbled for it on the beside drawers.

Ursula.

A quick glance at her clock told her she'd at least got a few hours of sleep—she'd gone to bed early and crashed immediately. It was one a.m., so five hours was a solid stretch, but not long enough for her. She was so tired she could sleep her life away.

She swiped the screen. "Yep."

"Sorry..."

"Doesn't matter. What's up?"

"Um, three bodies for you."

"Excuse me?" *What the fuck is up with this killer?*

"I know. Shocked me, too. Two women, one man. ID for all of them—but one might not be kosher. It's a name on one female's hand. None of them have been reported as missing."

Bethany wondered whether they'd be from the book club and steeled herself to hear names she didn't want to hear. "Who are they?"

"Male, Ian Stellar, fifty-one, clean record. Female, Clancy Robins, twenty-six—she's got previous for soliciting. Female, Jambrea Gaff, twenty-eight, clean record. She's the one with the name on her hand."

So not any of the book clubbers then. She didn't know whether to be relieved or not. Having met the clubbers, it would have been harder to bear, seeing their bodies. If it *had* been them, the connection and motive would eventually become clear, but now that it *wasn't* them, they were walking through a pea-soup fog, their direction well and truly obscured. "Okay. Do me a favour and ring Leona. Give her the names and addresses and ask her to do her usual digging when she gets to the station. What are their addresses, and who are the next of kin, please? Send them to me in a message after this call because I won't remember it all."

"Ian Stellar's NOK is his wife, Monica. Jambrea's is her mother—Jambrea lives with a man called Zac Ferguson."

Why do I know that name?

Ursula continued. "Clancy Robins is a different matter. Been through the foster system, parents deceased, both via drug overdoses. No children registered to Clancy, no known address since twenty-ten, but according to Tory Yates who called it in, Clancy lives in a druggy squat, but she doesn't know where."

"Right, where are the bodies?"

Ursula passed on that information, and Bethany reminded her to message everything to her, and ended the call. She phoned Mike, told him to get his arse out of bed, then nipped in the shower. She wasn't in there long, dressed quickly, made their usual coffees to-go, and was out on the road and to Mike's inside ten minutes.

What she wouldn't give for a sausage sarnie.

She informed Mike of what had happened, and they chatted about it on the journey, Mike incredulous that the killer had managed to murder without two of them kicking up a fuss and overpowering him when he concentrated on the third.

"Doesn't make sense," he said, "unless he tied them up."

"Might have been done elsewhere, one at a time, and the site is where he dumped them. We'll soon know. Presley will be able to tell us if they were murdered there."

She used the main road, then drove across a field once she spotted a SOCO van had done the same. It was parked in the distance, in front of one of four buildings. She recognised them as the old office blocks built around a square, their position much like the flaps of a cardboard box flattened out. It had been on the news recently that they had been acquired by some rich bloke or other to be renovated into flats. Wasn't that always the way of things these days? Housing and more housing? She hoped it would be affordable and not some trumped-up price that those on a budget couldn't afford—that was the type of homes needed, not all this posh, expensive stuff only available to the elite.

She stopped her car behind the SOCO van, which had one of the back doors open. They took the opportunity and used protective clothing from the boxes inside and, once covered from head to toe, they signed the log with Tory, who stood at the corner of the building.

"Go down there, and you'll see the courtyard," Tory said.

Bethany led the way, her stomach clenching, her mind conjuring up the horror she was about to see. Was it going to be weird, with the bodies all in a row, laid out like matches? She swallowed and walked out into the courtyard, her first impression stolen by the bright lights blaring in her eyes from the halogens that had been erected in every corner. Once her sight became accustomed, she had a nose around. One extra-large tent stood to the right by another building, and a second, smaller one, directly opposite the first, had been placed in front of a door.

Isabelle stood in the middle, having a conversation with a SOCO, four others on hands and knees around her. Bethany approached them, and Isabelle looked up.

"Ah, good morning, and we have a triple dose of gruesome today." Isabelle smiled, her face mask down by her chin. "Although there are some oddities this time. I have a theory. Let's start with the man first. Come on."

She walked off, and they followed her through the smaller tent and into the building. Another halogen illuminated the run-down room, what Bethany guessed had once been a reception area, because a curved desk stood to the right. A dead man was on the floor, his underwear and trousers at his ankles, one shoe off, one on, a toe missing, blood on the dirty floor but not as much as there should be. Bethany didn't bother roving her gaze upwards to see the rest of him. She needed a moment or two before that.

"Okay, oddity number one." Isabelle pointed. "A penis on the floor beside a condom."

Bethany didn't want a sausage sarnie anymore.

"Now, gross as this sounds, what's in the condom is still fluid, so pretty fresh," Isabelle continued. "My theory is he came here to have sex with the prostitute, Clancy Robins, and they were disturbed by the killer who was in the process of murdering Jambrea Gaff. Presley will shoot that theory out of the water, I'm sure, but that's my take on it at the moment. Now"—she aimed her finger at the dead man—"he was strangled. For some reason, his bruises have come up more pronounced compared to the other victims', so perhaps extra force was used with him. Dick removal—someone who shouldn't be using said dick to do certain things. We know damn well what cutting one off implies. He's either a sex pest or has been playing away. He has drawing pins in his belly, but they're a pattern this time. A smiley face. So, is the killer glad he's dead—more glad compared to the others? Who knows."

"Right." That was a lot to take in at once, so Bethany digested it for a few seconds. "He's got everything the same as the others?"

"Yes, all the same. Have a quick look then!" Isabelle sounded exasperated. "I really don't know why you hold off. Just rip the plaster away quickly, straight off the bat. Tormenting yourself with what you *might* see drives up the anxiety."

Bethany did so, and yes, he even had a tick on his forehead, although the depth didn't seem to be as much as the previous ones. She frowned. Opened her mouth to say something.

"Ah, you noticed that, too, did you?" Isabelle nodded to herself. "Maybe it's because he hasn't exactly got much fat on his brow."

"What are you on about?" Mike stepped closer.

"The depth of the tick," Isabelle said. "Not as much as before."

"Ah, I hadn't spotted that."

Isabelle went on. "Imagine—but not literally, because that's a bit pervy—this man here getting saucy with Clancy. He's done the deed—condom evidence, if it's even his—and they're disturbed by hearing the killer arrive with Jambrea. Clancy goes to the window. Look at it—someone's created a circle to peek through. There's a smear of blood on it as well. Hmm… Anyway, she sees Jambrea being strangled and rushes out there to help. The killer grabs Clancy, strangles her, too. Then he or she comes in here to check whether Clancy's customer is still around. Oh, there he is, lying in post-sex bliss, and he's strangled as well. Then the killer gets busy doing all the ticks, tacks, and toes, and leaves. But…there's something not sitting right with me regarding Ian here and Jambrea. Study him for a moment."

Isabelle folded her arms while Bethany ran her gaze up and down the body. Nothing stood out as particularly different apart from his missing penis, the tacks being a smiley face, and the minimal blood from where his toe used to be.

"See anything?" Isabelle raised her eyebrows.

Bethany shook her head but mentioned the toe blood.

"Then let's have a gander in the other tent so I can see if you pick up on it there instead."

A tad annoyed at Isabelle not just coming out with it, Bethany feeling inadequate and like she was being tested, they left the building and strode across the courtyard, dodging SOCO diligently searching for clues. Isabelle pulled the flap open and held it while Bethany and Mike went in.

The women's bodies weren't side by side exactly but close to each other, lending credence to Isabelle's theory. The blood from their toes being snipped off was significantly more here compared to Ian, although Jambrea's was slightly less than the other woman's, no spatter from pumping blood. Clancy's, as well as a pool of it, was widespread spatter where it had spurted in time with her heartbeats.

"I've got it," Bethany said. "Ian's toe was removed after he'd died. There isn't much mess, and the blood is thicker with him. Clancy's was removed while she was alive—look at the amount there is, how it's a pool plus copious spray. Jambrea's was also removed after death, but not long after because there's more blood than with Ian."

She noticed something else, too, and gave the women's faces a quick once-over. "The ticks on Ian and Jambrea were also done post death. Again, Jambrea's soon after as she at least has blood dribbles, just not as many as Clancy. Ian hardly has any, it's just ballooned up around the wound, so his blood was coagulating by the time his tick was made. He had to have been dead for fifteen minutes or more beforehand."

"Damn, I didn't catch that," Isabelle said. "I was focused on something else entirely."

"Hmm." Mike walked to the heads and crouched. "Clancy has a gun imprint on her temple. Jambrea doesn't, but I didn't think to check with Ian."

"That's what I was getting at." Isabelle stared into space. "And I've just realised that fucks my theory up."

Bethany nodded. "It does. Jambrea would have to be the one to have the gun imprint if she was the killer's actual target and Clancy came to help."

"Right, so did Jambrea come here with Ian and *Clancy* was the one being killed first? Did Jambrea come to her aid?" Isabelle sighed. "Balls. I thought I had it bang on as well." She looked a bit downcast. "Still, at least it wasn't Presley correcting me. He always comes off as smug when he does it."

"So who found them?" Bethany asked.

"Three homeless men. Now this is where it gets interesting," Isabelle said. "Earlier, about quarter to eight, a black-haired woman with glasses, dressed like a sex worker, according to them, came and gave them fifty pounds each to make themselves scarce. They were told to stay away for three hours. Of course, being given that much cash means they're going to go and get some food or whatever, which they did. They assumed she wanted the building Ian's in for conducting business. They use the second floor to live in and sex workers use the ground one."

"Won't be long before they're turfed out, what with these being turned into flats," Mike said, standing. "Wonder why they don't use the renovated warehouse behind the shelter? There's enough beds in there now for one hundred and sixty-two people. Did you hear the fund-raiser drive at Christmas ended up making ten grand?"

Isabelle nodded. "I did."

"But if you remember," Bethany said, "there were over two hundred homeless that we know of, and the spaces in the actual shelter, plus the ones in the warehouse, fall short of that number." She glanced at Isabelle. "So where are the three homeless men now?"

"They declined to stay and wait for you, even though Tory told them they weren't in any trouble."

"Don't suppose they gave their names?"

"No."

"So did they touch the bodies or anything?"

"They spotted the women and, believe it or not, admitted they ignored them and went straight into Ian's building. When they found him, though, they got the jitters, and one ran to the estate and asked a motorist to phone the police. That call can be traced to find out who it was."

Bethany sighed, the warm air hitting the inside of her face mask. "Fran or Leona can contact them. Well, we'll have to get on and see the next of kins—Ian's wife and Jambrea's mother. I suppose we ought to grab the chance now to visit the sex workers on their patch and see if any of them know Clancy and who she might have been meeting. We'll stop there on the way. Can you message me if Presley finds anything when he arrives and— Oh. There are dots on Clancy's stomach."

Isabelle laughed. "I was waiting for that. She'd had tacks put there, then they were removed. If you notice, Ian and Jambrea don't have many, so I really do believe the killer wasn't expecting to off more than one person and only brought enough tacks for, let's say Clancy. The amount of dots she has matches the amount of tacks in Ian and

Jambrea." She took a deep breath, then let it out slow and steady, as if it calmed her. "There's something else you need to look at. The grid."

Bethany and Mike moved over to it, both staring down.

"Ticks five and six aren't chalk," Mike said.

So true. Four crosses were thick, as if those fat sticks of chalk had been used, but five and six were thin. A stone about the size of a golf ball sat in box seven.

"His chalk ran out?" Even as she said it, Bethany knew that wasn't right.

"I'm saying two killers." Isabelle.

"Or maybe one killer, but they used the stone on purpose, so the cross wasn't as thick, showing us those people weren't as important as the others?" Mike offered.

"God knows. Whatever it is, my head's screwed," Bethany said. "Once Presley has time of death estimates, let me know if we're not back here by then, okay? The order of deaths could be crucially important here." Bethany rolled her shoulders. "We need to get going. Tarra for now."

They walked to where Tory stood, signed the log, and disposed of their protectives. In the car, she processed the information bit by bit as she took them to the sex worker patch closest to the crime scene. It was on the outer edge of the estate.

Two women waited for customers.

Bethany pulled up. "Stay in the car. Both of us approaching is likely to spook them. Open your window, though, and write down what they say."

CHAPTER SIXTEEN

Bethany joined the women on the path.
"Are you wanting a threesome, love?" one
asked. Blonde. Around thirty. "That's three
times the fee. More risk, see."

Bethany smiled. "No. Before I go on, I'm a police
officer—no, please, don't walk away. Someone has

been killed, and I need to know if you knew her."
She showed them her ID. "I'm DI Bethany Smith. I
absolutely don't care at this moment what you're
doing here."

"Killed? Was it one of us?" The brunette's eyes
widened.

"I don't know if it's one of your friends who
might usually be on this patch or if she's from
another," Bethany said. "This one is closest to the
murder site, so that's why we're here. Do you
know Clancy Robins?"

"*She's* dead?" The blonde.

"I'm afraid so. She was murdered."

"By that nutter going around?" Blondie again,
mouth hanging open. She thrust a hand in her
small bag, brought out a vape, and sucked on it.

"Yes. Have you seen her recently?"

"She went off with a punter about half eight."
Blondie.

"Give us a bit of that." Brunette took the vape
and chugged on it, blowing out strawberry-
scented smoke.

"Did you recognise him?" Bethany asked.

Blondie shook her head. "No, but she did say:
Oh God, not him. What does he want?"

"So she knew him," Bethany thought out loud.

Blondie shrugged and took the vape back from
her friend. "Seemed like it to me, but I've not seen
him stopping here before. Black car, but then most
are, so maybe he *has* been here and I just haven't
spotted him. One punter said it's because black

becomes invisible and the police take no notice when men kerb-crawl."

Could it be Ian's car? Shit. I should have asked Ursula to check what make he has. "Does the name Ian Stellar mean anything to you?"

Blondie gasped. "*Ian*? I went with him earlier."

Bethany's heart leapt. "You did? What time?"

"I have to meet him every week at eight, but I was a couple of minutes late. I walked over the field there." She jerked a thumb behind her.

Bethany looked past Blondie's shoulder. The old office blocks were back there. A square of light from the halogens in the courtyard appeared eerie from here, a patch in the darkness, although that would be obliterated soon. Morning light was creeping up the horizon as a light-grey line. "So you went and met him *there*?" She pointed at the buildings.

"Yeah." Blondie turned to stare. "I left here, walked across the field, and was gawping at a car parked behind the building on the left. It wasn't Ian's, so I got a bit cautious. Thought he'd done the dirty on me and brought someone else along without asking me first—he's mentioned a threesome, see. I decided to go round the building on the right, all the way past the one at the back, and check the car to the left. No one was in it, but the bonnet was warm—I put my hand on it—so I knew someone was about. I went to the block at the back, because that's where I always go with Ian, and his car was there. I met him, relieved he hadn't brought a mate, did the usual, then came back here."

"What time was that?"

"About twenty-five past eight maybe? Then, just as I arrived here, Clancy got picked up by the fella in the black car."

"I just need to message my colleague about Ian's vehicle. Two secs." Bethany did that, telling Isabelle to look for it at the scene and check with Ursula whether it was his, although it may have already been found and Isabelle had forgotten to mention it. She gave the blonde her attention again. "Did you see anyone else there before you left? In the courtyard perhaps?"

She shook her head. "No. I ran across the field to catch another customer who'd parked up and was waiting. With Clancy gone, I bagged him for myself. I got in his car. He took me somewhere, and by the time I got back, the vehicle that'd been parked, the one I just told you about with the warm bonnet, was gone."

"What colour was it?"

"Red."

"The make?"

"No idea. But it came back again, though, didn't notice the time. I was by myself and turned to watch whoever it was get out. They went down the side of the building, stayed out of sight for a few minutes, then reappeared, going to the boot. They took something big out and carried it down beside the block."

Bethany got butterflies. "Did you see them clearly?"

"From this distance? God, no."

"Which direction did they come from when they arrived?"

"They were driving in from the main road and cut across the field."

Shit. So they'd parked close to where Bethany had, by the SOCO van and Tory's patrol. "Did you see them leave?"

"No, I got another customer."

"Did *you* see?" Bethany looked at Brunette.

"No, I was lucky enough to cop a stint with three blokes about twenty past eight. I went to their house. They dropped me back here about eleven, so I missed everything."

"Thank you *very* much for your time. You've been more helpful than you know. Please be careful out here, though, and be mindful of who you go with. If you see that red car come back or the black one Clancy got in, please ring me—and *do not* go with them, understand?" She handed them a card each. "Would you be willing to give me your names?"

They shook their heads. She understood why they'd refused. They might have children, family members who didn't know what they did at night.

"If I need you in court, would you be up for getting involved then?"

Again, head shakes.

She left them there, stomach queasy in case the murderer came back and decided to kill them, too, tying up loose ends.

In the car, she was about go over everything with Mike, but her phone beeped the message tone.

Isabelle: IT'S HERE. URSULA DID A CHECK ON IT FOR ME. THE VEHICLE BELONGS TO IAN.

Bethany: OKAY, THE GIRLS ALSO TOLD ME A CAR HAD PARKED WHERE THE SOCO VAN IS. GET IT MOVED, FARTHER BACK, THE PATROL CAR, TOO, SO INSPECTIONS CAN BE DONE FOR TYRE TRACKS AND WHATNOT.

Isabelle: SHIT, WE COULD HAVE FUCKED THAT RIGHT UP BY LEAVING OUR VEHICLES THERE.

Bethany: I KNOW, BUT DON'T WORRY ABOUT THAT NOW. I NEED TO CONTACT LEONA REGARDING CCTV, SO CATCH YOU LATER.

She did that, then opened the message Ursula had sent earlier with the next of kin information. "Jambrea's mother or Ian's wife first?"

"The wife." He nudged her. "Out with it. What's going on? I couldn't hear much of what you and the women talked about."

She started the engine and headed towards Ian Stellar's address. Everything came out in a rush she was that excited to have something to go on, and he asked her to repeat it, slowly.

Once she had, she said, "We could *definitely* be talking two killers here. Not only because of the chalk being wrong but because of the man who picked Clancy up. We know Ian had already had intercourse with the blonde sex worker I spoke to.

Killer number one was at the scene—we assume, because of the red car being present—while Blondie did what she did with Ian. Blondie then returned to the patch. Killer number two, the punter in the black car, picked Clancy up and took her to the blocks. Killer one, and Ian, were still there. Was Jambrea taken out of that boot later on and carried into the courtyard? Why go off and come back with another body? What the *fuck* went on?"

"I need to write this all down in a timeline to get it straight in my head." Mike got his notebook out and spoke each point as he wrote. "Okay, clear as mud."

She smiled and turned into Ian's road. The houses were in darkness, but one wasn't—and it just happened to be his. Light spilled through the opaque glass in the top of the front door, plus it glowed behind cream curtains in the window beside it. Was Monica Stellar in there, waiting for her husband to come home?

They knocked, and a woman answered, the opposite to Blondie in every way. Assuming it was Monica, she was elegant to the point of bringing on a twinge of envy. It was clear she had her shit together—lovely dark hair and red nails, her black clothing expensive. So she hadn't got ready for bed—too worried to do so? Her makeup was perfect, going down the less-is-more route. She appeared well-tended, but that could all change soon. Tears liked to wreck makeup.

Bethany held up her ID. "I'm DI Bethany Smith, and this is my partner, DS Mike Wilkins. Monica Stellar? We're here regarding your husband, Ian."

"But I haven't reported him missing yet," she said quietly.

"May we come in?"

Monica stepped back into a large hallway, and once Bethany and Mike were inside, she closed the door, leading them into the living room. A throw cushion rested against the arm of the sofa and had a head dent in it, as though she had been lying down. She plumped it up and set it to one side, then sat.

"Please, take a seat," she said.

Bethany picked a chair by the door, and Mike stood beside it.

"You said you haven't reported him missing yet," Bethany said. "When was he supposed to get home?"

"Maybe about eleven, when the pub shuts. He goes out every week. Says he has a regular meeting with a client at eight, then he has a few drinks."

That tied in with Blondie's account of her being with him.

"What client is this?" Bethany asked, trying to get a clue as to whether Monica was aware her husband visited a sex worker.

Monica wrung her hands. "Someone to do with the business, I don't know who."

"What business is that?"

"He owns Stellar Mini-Mart."

Ah, that was where Bethany had heard the name before. The penny had dropped way too late. "Okay. Is it usual for weekly meetings in the evening with a client? In his line of business, I mean. Why can't that be conducted during the daytime?"

"I don't know. He doesn't tell me much."

I bet he bloody didn't. "Is the client a man or a woman?"

"I don't know that either."

"What did you think when he didn't come home at his usual time?"

"Maybe that the meeting went on for longer and they decided to stay for a lock-in or something. Or even go to a club." She glanced at the clock on the wall behind her. "It's half two. He might be home any minute."

"Does the name Clancy Robins mean anything to you?"

Monica shook her head. "Maybe she's the client."

She was certainly something... "Does your husband have any enemies?"

Another head shake. "None he's told me about."

"What sort of man is he?"

"Kind, considerate." A flinch, one that wouldn't be seen by someone not trained to spot it. Did that mean she'd told a lie? "But he sometimes gets a little...loud. We all have rows, don't we?"

"We do. What time did he leave for this meeting?"

213

"I don't know. I wasn't home. I was having my nails done." She held them up.

"Where was this?"

"Tips and Talons. They're open until nine this evening." She blushed. "I mean last night. I forgot it's the early hours of the morning for a moment there."

"What time did you get back?"

"Eight."

"Can anyone verify that?"

Monica nodded. "Yes, I went with my next-door neighbour at number twelve. She had her nails done pink."

"Is she a good friend?"

She nodded again. "We've become close over the past few months, since just after she moved in."

"Would she be willing to come round here and sit with you?"

Monic frowned. "What for? Ian will be back soon."

"He won't, Mrs Stellar."

"I don't understand." She looked from Bethany to Mike then back again. "Has he done something wrong? Is that why you're here, to tell me you arrested him? Did he get involved in a fight at the pub, is that it?"

Why would she think that if he's kind and considerate? Did loud people get into fights regularly? "No. I'm sorry, Mrs Stellar, but your husband's body was found a short while ago."

214

"W-what? His b-b-body?" She lifted her hand to her mouth, eyes glistening. "He's...he's dead?"

Bethany nodded. "I'm afraid so. He was murdered."

"Pardon?" Her hand shook as she lowered it to her lap. "Who would want to do that? Did he get stabbed at the pub?" The tears fell, and her lips went wonky.

"No, we believe he was killed by the person who has committed the murders around here recently."

Monica's eyebrows shot up, as though she found that news utterly unbelievable. "By the person carving those foreheads and...and doing all those other horrible things?" She paled and appeared to have trouble taking it in, as if that couldn't possibly be the truth.

"Yes. Shall we get that neighbour for you now?"

Monica was apparently too stunned to cry properly. But that would come later. Sometimes, this kind of news took a while to register.

They didn't stay after her friend appeared—yes, she had pink nails; yes, she'd been to Tips and Talons with Monica. There was time enough for Bethany and Mike to come back and speak to Monica another day. After her refusal to have Alice Jacobs round for a chat, they departed, back in the car to visit Jambrea's mother.

She took the news terribly and didn't have a clue why her daughter might be targeted.

"I only spoke to her yesterday morning, so she can't be dead. It was just before she went on a run. She'd complained of having migraines for the past couple of days and thought a jog might help clear her mind. How do you know it's her?"

"Her name was written on her hand."

"That could be anything! What about her tattoo?"

"What's it of?"

The mother explained. Bethany got hold of Isabelle to check. Sadly, the images matched.

They left her mum with a relative and Alice Jacobs' number. From there, they went to Jambrea's home address. A man opened the door, his hair dishevelled, his face showing signs of him having broken sleep. He blinked when Bethany introduced them, as if he'd been expecting their arrival but hadn't believed they'd actually turn up to confirm that his worst fears had come true.

"Zac Ferguson, yes?" She remembered then why his name rang a bell. He'd been to collect books at Bertram's flat. Now wasn't exactly the time to question him about that, though.

"He nodded, invited them into his kitchen, and offered them a drink. Bethany and Mike accepted.

While he made the coffees, he said, "I didn't know when the right time was to ring up and say she was missing. Twenty-four hours before your lot will act, isn't it? I mean, she went out for a jog this morning—well, yesterday morning now— must have been about eleven, give or take. I remember thinking she was gone a fair while and that maybe she'd nipped to see a friend. I checked the house, and she'd left her bag and purse here, but her phone was gone, which is normal. She takes it with her in case, you know. Loads of weirdoes about. Anyway, I rang her a few times, messaged her as well, and then I got to thinking I'd better go out and look for her. I drove around for a while at lunchtime, didn't see her, so came home. I went out a bit later as well, arrived back here around half eight, something like that. We've been sniping at each other lately, so I assumed she'd gone off for a bit of me time."

He handed out their drinks.

"Thank you," Bethany said. "What happened then?"

"I fell asleep. I was going to phone her mum, see, but that was a last resort because she doesn't like me. Anyway, like I said, I dropped off to sleep, then you came."

"Do you know of anyone who would want to harm her?"

"Eh?" He frowned at them over the rim of his cup. Took a sip. "Jambrea? Nope. Why? Has something happened to her?"

"I'm very sorry, but her body was found earlier."

He'd just swallowed more coffee and choked. Mike took the cup off him and placed it on the worktop so it didn't spill everywhere.

Zac stared at them in turn, his bottom lip wobbling. "*Jambrea*? Are you sure?"

"We weren't at first. All we had to go on was her name written on her hand, but her mother said she had a tattoo, and we confirmed with the lead scene of crime officer that they matched."

Zac staggered to the table and flumped into a chair. He stared at the wall, blinking, shaking his head. "I-I don't get it. Who did it?"

"We think she was killed by the same person who's been committing the murders the past few days. Have you heard about those?"

He sucked in a breath and gripped the table edge. "*What?*" He turned to look at them, his face drained of colour. "It can't be... She... I was supposed to..."

"I know this is distressing, and I'm truly sorry you're going through this, but the key elements are in place, so it's probably the same killer." While she didn't know that for sure, and they suspected a second murderer was in play, she wouldn't muddy the waters here at the moment. It was difficult enough for the poor man to accept as it was.

"I read it in the paper. Tick, tack...t-t-toe?" he said, each word rising in pitch.

"Yes."

He gazed at the tabletop, still holding on for dear life. "How could it have happened when I...? How...?"

"Do you know a Clancy Robins?"

"No." Monotone.

"Ian Stellar?"

"No!" Incredulous.

"Do you need company for after we leave, Mr Ferguson?"

He ran his shaking hands through his hair. "Did they...did they carve her forehead and c-cut her...her toe off?"

"Yes."

"It should have been me," he wailed.

God, how sad. "It's natural for you to wish you could take her place," Bethany said. "It's instinct to wish it had been you and not her. You love her, so you wouldn't want this to happen to her."

They were all silent for a while, Bethany and Mike drinking their coffees. Then Zac cleared his throat.

"Where was she? Where did you find her?"

"At the abandoned office blocks on the edge of the city."

"What?" It came out as a squeak.

"Clancy Robins and Ian Stellar were also killed and left at the same location, which is why I asked if you knew them."

"Oh God, the grid..." He covered his face with his hands.

Bloody Peter Uxbridge, making all this information common knowledge. "Yes, that was there. The killer has marked six crosses now, so we're desperate to find whoever it is before the other three get filled in. If you can think of anyone lately who Jambrea might have discussed with you as bothering her or acting oddly..."

"Six?" He sobbed then, resting his head on his folded hands on the table. "Nine. Nine."

"Yes, there are nine boxes altogether."

It took fifteen minutes for him to calm down enough that they could leave—they had a duty of care to ensure he was all right. He assured them everything was okay, he'd manage, and they walked out.

Next stop, going back to the scene and seeing if Presley had arrived.

He was there, but so was that sodding Uxbridge, parked a few metres away from the now moved SOCO van and patrol car.

She approached his vehicle. The driver's-side window was open, and she bent over to glare inside. "Leave."

He pulled his gaze from Tory ahead. "Oh. It's you. Might have known *you'd* turn up to shoo me away."

"Do you have any idea of the *shit* you've caused by printing all those details in your bloody article?"

He shrugged. "It's my job. Told you before. Get over it."

"Off this crime scene. Now."

Uxbridge laughed. "Knickers. In. A. Twist."

He reversed at speed, and she waited until he'd driven off on the main road. She got dressed and signed the log, then caught up with Mike, who was already in protectives, talking to a SOCO, and they trudged back to the courtyard, Bethany fuming from her encounter with that hateful reporter.

No morals or empathy, that one.

A chat with Presley revealed his estimates regarding times of death, but they were so close, he gave his guess that the murders went in order of Ian, Clancy, and Jambrea.

Bethany and Mike then returned to the station, where they trawled through CCTV in an attempt to spot the black car, and the red one.

It was going to be a long few hours. Maybe they'd manage a nap before the rest of the team came in. She could only hope.

CHAPTER SEVENTEEN

Zac had slept fitfully, waking at ten a.m., still angry that someone was pretending to be him. And how the fuck had they known to take their victims *there*, where he'd left Clancy? Had they been following him? Was the old gang from his childhood spying on him after all, when they'd agreed not to do that? *And* someone had filled in two squares of his grid, the cheeky bastards.

That unsettled his chi or whatever the hell it was called.

He'd have to have a cuppa in a minute to calm down.

He switched on his phone and accessed *The Shadwell Herald* site, eager to know what the police knew about him.

With Jambrea dead, he was out of sorts. He'd nearly slipped up with those coppers, saying that he was supposed to be the one to kill her. He'd babbled "Nine. Nine..." and had to catch himself from saying that was her number. Thank God Smith had thought something else when he'd said "It should have been me!" or whatever it was he'd mumbled. Close call or what.

That bloody woman of his. She'd been a thorn in his side the past couple of years—a long and painful one that twisted about and angered him. And who was going to be his number nine now? No way was he accepting responsibility for the bloke who was offed, although by rights, he should have been on Zac's list, but Susan had annoyed him more, so she'd taken his place when he'd sat there choosing his victims. And Jambrea wasn't his anymore, so he wasn't getting the blame for her either. But the prosser, yes, he knew her all right.

He sighed and concentrated on reading.

MORE BODIES – THE COUNT RISES!

PETER UXBRIDGE – REGIONAL CRIME

Yesterday afternoon, year six schoolchildren made a gruesome find in the copse behind Westlake Allotments. An elderly gentleman, Bert Yawling, had been murdered in the same manner as the other victims reported in *The Herald* this week. This was shocking, coming on the back of Susan Burrow and Keith Crow losing their lives. But brace yourselves, that's not all...

Last night, other bodies were left for members of the public to find. Yes, you read that right. Is this the killer's aim? Do they want innocent people to happen upon corpses? It seems so. Three homeless men stumbled on two women at the old Mintwell office blocks. They had been left in the courtyard, and the same pattern was followed—ticks carved into foreheads, tacks pressed into stomachs, and toes cut off and inserted into navels. The females were Jambrea Gaff and Clancy Robins.

What is going on, you ask? More. There's more. A male was then discovered in one of the office blocks. Ian Stellar of Stellar Mini-Mart also fell foul of the same killer—and sources say he'd been at the scene to meet with a sex worker. Oh, the plot thickens...

Someone is on a rampage, and the police need to up the ante if they're going to stop that game grid being completely filled with the sinister chalk crosses. Who will be next?

Our main source said:

"It is imperative that the public remains vigilant. As I've stressed many times before, changes in behaviour are not uncommon when someone embarks on a killing spree, so if anybody you know is acting differently, in a way that gives you cause for concern, contact the police immediately. Even if you think you're wasting our time, you won't be. All leads will be investigated."

We at *The Herald* have yet more shocking news for you. A gun was used to threaten the victims. However, the imprint where it was pressed into temples and backs doesn't match any gun the police are familiar with. So, has it been smuggled into the country?

A disturbing nugget of information, isn't it?

We'll update as soon as we know anything new. Stay tuned, folks, and be careful. It's a minefield out there. Our town, formerly known as Shadwell, should be renamed Serial—the place where killers are born.

Chilling!

That was bullshit. Zac hadn't planned for the public to find the bodies at all. He hadn't even thought about what happened afterwards. He was only interested in killing them, getting them out of his life. That *Herald* fella was talking out of his windbag arse.

Zac thought about when he'd picked Clancy up. He'd smeared dirt on his number plates—like he was going to chance CCTV catching it on tape—and parked on the other side of the road from where she'd stood with some other tart. She'd got in, no problem, and sat beside him.

Back when he'd helped rob the shop, Clancy had held one of the fake guns to the owner's head. Yeah, she'd got into his car all right, too scared to do otherwise. And as for one of the victim's being Ian Stellar, fucking hell. That was just plain creepy.

"Go, go, go!" Pig said at the door of Stellar Mini-Mart, the snout of his mask wobbling.

They burst inside, Cow and Donkey turning right to sort the old dear standing there screaming with her wire basket, plus some middle-aged woman with her three bratty kids. Pig went straight for the alcohol fridge, as planned, his holdall zip already open. Clancy the Chicken stood by the till, Sheep ran down to stuff his rucksack with whatever expensive stuff he could grab so they could sell it on, and Zac the Gorilla kept guard by the door. He drew the blind down over it. There were that many posters advertising Buy One Get One Free over the other windows, no one would be able to see inside between them unless they pressed their nose to the glass.

Old Biddy and the children screamed and snivelled, while Mother Hen assured the kids everything would be all right, and it would. They hadn't planned on hurting anyone. They just wanted booze, fags, shit to flog, and money. Nothing excessive.

"Shut your fucking mouth, Granny!" Pig shouted in The Voice of Fear. "And keep those brats quiet or I'll fucking blow their brains out. One more word, and you're toast."

Zac couldn't see him—Pig was two aisles over—but those last few words... God, Zac wished it'd been him who'd said them. Yeah, these people would be toast if they didn't do as they were told.

"Because if you don't do what I said, I'm not messing, I'll use this gun," Pig went on.

"You'd better listen," Sheep called.

"I'm ringing the police," Mr Stellar said.

That had Zac's guts rolling over. He looked at the shop owner, who stood like a right dickhead with his hands above his head. Chicken Clancy had her gun pointed at him, her hand shaking, the stupid bitch. She was giving away how scared she was— that or she was coming down off her spliff high. Zac knew they shouldn't have included her, but she was in their gang and had recently started taking harder drugs and needed money for her fixes. Fifteen years old and hooked, the scummy bint.

"Fucking ring the coppers, and Chicken will shoot," Pig said, coming over and dumping the holdall beside the counter. The bottles clanked inside. "Now put fags in there, some spirits. Do it."

Mr Stellar did as he'd been told, turning to the shelving behind him, ignoring the spirits. Chicken poked the muzzle into his temple at one point. Again, Zac wished it was him who was in the thick of it instead of standing there as a bloody lookout—he'd love to jam a gun to Stellar's head like that. Even Cow and Donkey were having a better time of it, Cow with his arm across Old Biddy's neck, Donkey waving a fake rifle around near Mother Hen and the kids. Sheep was doing God knew what, but it had to be better than being a lemon like Zac.

Mr Stellar added another pack of two hundred Bensons to the holdall. "There's no more room."

"Then give us the money from the till," Pig demanded. "Open it." He waggled his gun.

Mr Stellar did so with a tap on a keypad, then he handed over a wedge of tenners. Pig stuffed them in his pocket. As Stellar was about to grab the twenties, Zac remembered he had a job to do and peered out of the door by holding the blind back a bit.

"Company coming," he said. "One minute, tops."

Pig zipped the holdall then scooped it up. Sheep appeared, slinging his backpack on. Cow shoved Old Biddy, who fell into a stack of cornflakes, landing on her back on the floor, her basket contents plunking on top of her. The edge of that can of beans had to have stung the way it walloped her chin. The actual basket crashed onto her head. She stared though the wire mesh, crying. Donkey whacked Mother Hen in the face with the rifle, and the kids screamed.

"Fucking noisy shits," Pig snarled. "What did I tell you about shutting up?"

"No, no, please, not my kids," Mother Hen whimpered.

"You're lucky we need to get out of here," Pig said. "Otherwise, you'd all be dead, motherfuckers."

Donkey wet himself laughing at that, and Sheep joined in, their wheezy chuckles strange from behind their masks. Zac moved away from the door, ready to open it, desperate to leg it, and Chicken once again pressed the muzzle to Mr Stellar's temple and pushed it, hard. He stumbled, and an angry red indent had imprinted on his skin.

Zac would remember that forever.

"I'll come back and kill you," Chicken said, forgetting to use The Voice of Fear.

"Clancy Robins?" Old Biddy shrieked. "Is that you?"

Fuck. Now look what's happened.

Zac swung the door wide and went to go outside, but Clancy and Pig barged past him, exiting, the holdall bumping into Zac's stomach and nudging him into the little metal shelves of Wrigley's chewing gum on the counter. Donkey, Cow, and Sheep came next, the gang giggling their heads off outside. Then Zac burst through the doorway, laughing himself through nerves until—

"Fuck, get off me!" he said, The Voice of Fear deep.

That Keith Crow bloke had come along, had hold of him by his collar, and Zac had never felt so scared in his life. The gang hadn't noticed and were still laughing, going on about what was stolen and how pissed they could all get on the booze.

"Help me!" Zac shouted to them.

But they ran off. They fucking ran off, for God's sake, leaving him with Keith.

Bloody hell, bloody hell...

"You ever do anything like this again, I'll fucking have you," Keith said, right in Zac's ear.

He let Zac go. Zac ran after his mates, adrenaline flashing through his system. They'd gone round the corner. He caught up with them, and they kept going, running so fast until they reached the river over a mile away. They stood by the wooden bench and dumped the masks in the water, watching them float off, jostling with the current, a wild bunch of animals, just like their wearers.

"Why did you leave me?" Zac asked, sweat pouring down his face. The scent of latex from the mask clung to his skin.

"Because we'd have got caught an' all," Pig said. "Better that it was just one of us."

Zac vowed there and then to get them back. He'd never forgive them for this.

The next day, someone killed Old Biddy by staving her head in, but Clancy swore it wasn't her. Who else would it have been, though? Hers was the only name mentioned in the shop. She was the only one who had something to fear.

That afternoon, Mother Hen's house burnt down from a petrol-soaked rag in the letterbox, her and the kids inside. Fuck, Zac had felt a bit sick over that, but Bert Yawling had soon taken his mind off it with his constant use of a place on Zac's body he shouldn't have been touching.

Then there was Mr Stellar—why hadn't he been killed? Zac found out Clancy had offered him a few shags to stop him telling anyone she'd been one of the robbers, and he'd bloody well taken her up on it. But Stellar gave Zac funny looks every time he went in the shop, as though he knew Zac had been involved, too.

"If I find out it was you, there'll be trouble," Stellar said while taking the money for the Twirl Zac was buying.

"I don't know what you're on about," Zac said in his normal voice.

"Yes, you do. I'll be watching you, boy."

Life was shit, it really was, and Zac went off the rails a bit. Not surprising, with what he was going through. People were dead because they'd robbed Stellar. Because Clancy had forgotten to use The Voice of Fear. Stellar was just waiting to catch Zac out. Then there was Bert. Zac's parents, oblivious, too interested in their own lives to notice the shite going on in his.

With a screwed-up mind, Zac plodded on and did his best to forget everything.

It was all he could do, wasn't it?

Zac wiped his eyes, angry at how the past still affected him. No wonder he'd ended up mixing with the likes of Erica Orloff as an adult, robbing that old dear of her savings, and setting up a money-lending business after years of drifting in and out of cruddy work, being on Jobseeker's a lot of the time. When he'd met Jambrea, she'd been after a bad boy, so she'd said, and his reputation had come before him, so she'd chosen him. Then she'd expected him to change, do things her way, and moaned all the while. And now she was dead, not by his hand, and it rankled.

Nothing ever went his way.

Well, from now on, it would. He'd just have to be careful with the next four, which would make eight kills. Then again, if he did the four today, earlier than planned, while the police were still wrapped up with the other murders, they wouldn't be that interested in him being Jambrea's other half. That left her spot on the grid open, but there was nothing he could do about that.

With the small baggie of Lenny's gear in his pocket, he'd use it to his advantage. All right, it meant his plan deviated a bit, but that was okay. A change was as good as a rest and all that.

He left the house and drove to the mini phone box library on the outskirts. It was out of the way there so he could do what he had to, and because the road was rarely used, he'd see cars coming a mile off. He put gloves on to use a burner phone to text Pig, Cow, Sheep, and Donkey, so he could tell them he needed to meet them all—now. They'd shit themselves and think it was about the robbery, and wouldn't news of that leaking out fuck up their now perfect lives with their pretty wives and gorgeous children? They'd agreed, when they'd turned eighteen, to part ways, never to get in contact again unless it was trouble regarding Stellar Mini-Mart—and also to always inform each other when their mobile numbers changed.

Zac knew theirs off by heart.

Zac: IT'S GORILLA. LOST MY NORMAL PHONE. WE NEED TO MEET. PROBLEM. BE AT THE RIVER IN THIRTY. NO EXCUSES.

Pig: WTF?

Cow: YOU WHAT?

Donkey: CHRIST, I DON'T NEED THIS.

Sheep: PLEASE DON'T TELL ME IT'S COME HOME TO ROOST.

Zac: IT HAS. THE SHIT IS ABOUT TO HIT THE FAN, SO I SUGGEST YOU DO AS I SAID. I'LL BRING BEER. YOU'LL NEED IT.

He removed the SIM, cleaned the phone on his T-shirt, got out of the car, and stamped on the burner. He wedged the SIM behind one of the shelves in the phone box. Scooped the phone debris up and lobbed it into the nearby field. Then he drove off to Stellar Mini-Mart for old time's sake, to buy the beer. It was open, despite the wanker being dead, and the usual drippy woman he employed stood behind the counter, the scutty mare. She had about eight kids and didn't wash, so the rumours said. Going by the state of her hair, that was true.

Back in his Golf, he drove to the river, parking as close to their spot as he could. While he waited, he sat on the bench, the same one they'd always sat on while smoking, drinking, and having a laugh as youngsters, and opened four cans of Fosters. He poured some out of each, onto the grass, in case the gear made it froth. Then he sprinkled more than the tip of a teaspoon in each one. And no, it didn't froth.

The sound of a car engine drew his attention. An SUV parked beside his car, and Pig, Cow, Sheep, and Donkey got out. Nice. They all must still keep in touch, otherwise, why were they together? Unless they'd arranged this when Zac had ditched his phone.

Whatever.

They came up to him, giving him evils, and he handed out the beers as though their hatred didn't hurt him. *Why* did they hate him, though? For getting them here like this?

He hoped they didn't notice the cans felt a bit lighter than usual. "You'll need one of these before I tell you. I opened them ready, see."

All four of them swigged. Zac opened a fifth. Drank a mouthful. His so-called mates from days gone by chugged the cans quickly. That hadn't changed then.

None of them spoke, so Zac got on with it.

"Clancy's been murdered," he said. "And Stellar."

"I saw it online." Pig shrugged. "Who cares about that junkie bitch anyway? I've never forgiven her for opening her gob. And Stellar, that's good, isn't it? Saves us having to worry about him identifying us. He's always looked at me funny since that night. Told me once he knew it was us. We were stupid to think he wouldn't.

235

Everyone round there knew we all hung out together."

Cow and Donkey agreed. Sheep nodded, and that name suited him. He always had followed along with whatever the others said or did. Zac felt a bit better about Stellar saying the same stuff to Pig. At least it wasn't just Zac the shopkeeper had scared shitless.

"Seems that mad killer had a problem with Clancy and Stellar as well as us," Cow said, burping the last two words. He always was a dirty fucker.

"Yeah," Donkey said. "I did wonder if it was one of us, but that old pervert bloke, the Crow fella, and the library woman didn't make sense." He swayed, as if he'd had more than a can.

The gear's working.

"Who killed Old Biddy, Mother Hen, and the kids?" Zac asked.

None of them answered. They looked shamefaced, though, so one of them had done it. Maybe all of them. They'd left him out of that bloody job, and he was glad.

"You bastards," Zac said. "How could you off *children*?"

"Shit, I don't feel right," Pig said.

"Me neither." Cow.

"You should all feel sick if you were involved in killing those people, the granny and whatever," Zac said, ignoring the fact *he* didn't feel guilty for what he'd done. "And as for Clancy and Stellar..." Long pause for effect. "What if we're next?"

236

He enjoyed the expressions of fear that swarmed their faces.

"Fuck off," Donkey slurred. He staggered then fell, landing on his arse.

Sheep followed him down.

"What's up with them?" Pig, frowning.

Then Pig and Cow keeled over, and the gear had done its job. Zac was the last one standing from their gang, and that was bittersweet justice, that was. They'd viewed him as the weakest of them all when they were kids, and now look at him, the strongest of the lot. He stared down at them while they tried to speak, and within ten minutes, they were out of it.

He crunched up the cans and dropped them in the footwell of his car—they couldn't be left behind, they had his fingerprints on them. Next, he collected his kill bag from the boot and got on with the job. It was daylight, and he had to put a rush on. Some random fisherman could come along, or a stupid mother with her nippers, out to feed the ducks.

An hour later, he drew the grid on the bench, filling in eight squares. The police would be scratching their heads. The crosses wouldn't match what they were expecting, seeing as that other killer had added two last time.

Good. Let them wonder.

He drove away, glad everyone was gone now. He'd have to learn not to allow anyone to piss him off in future. He'd done what he'd set out to do, and this was the end of it. Mind you, that last

237

square being empty dogged him off, nagged at him, and he searched his mind for one more person, just so he'd filled in the whole thing.

Jambrea's mum? She'd do, wouldn't she?

On the way to his house, he travelled past the allotment, testing his courage being so near to a crime scene. A kid caught his eye. She zoomed towards him on her pink-and-white bike, blonde ponytail on top of her head this time, streaming behind her she was speeding that fast. She turned onto the track, probably going home via the field, and he took a big risk, driving down there after her. She veered left at the end, and he followed, watching her as she disappeared into the copse where he'd first seen her. No police, they'd long gone, but a piece of crime scene tape had been left tied around a tree trunk and hung limply, useless.

He remembered what he'd said to the gang. About killing children.

And ignored it.

Parked inside the copse, he wound down his side window and stared through the windscreen. She stopped, turned to look over her dainty shoulder. Her eyes widened—*she's registered who I am.*

"You're that bad man," she said and scrabbled on the pedals, eager to get away, one foot slipping, the toe of her pretty white sandal digging into the patchy grass.

Zac had done the right thing in following her. She knew who he was. He got out, leaving the engine running so it'd disguise any noise. She pushed off on her bike, moving away. He jogged up behind her. The small tyres and stabilisers couldn't take her as fast over the uneven ground. He snatched her ponytail and lifted her clean off that bike, and she dangled, him holding her up, her body swinging round so she faced him, her mouth opening, ready for her to scream.

"Hello, Box Number Nine."

Then he clamped her narrow, fragile little back to his chest, slapped a hand over her mouth, and got to work.

CHAPTER EIGHTEEN

Erica had made the final decision. She'd kill Lenny. He really was pushing it with those sexy videos. Why did he feel the need to keep watching them? She clearly wasn't enough for him. The thing was, she didn't have the energy needed to strangle him, not after killing Stellar and

Jambrea, so she'd ask him along to her next job and bump him off afterwards. He'd jump at the chance of getting in on the action, seeing how she worked.

He will be seeing it up close and personal.

Some man wanted his son killed. She had to meet the father later at their prearranged spot. Her client had contacted her months ago and should have saved the money in dribs and drabs by now. He'd originally wanted to do a direct bank transfer, the stupid weasel.

She wondered how many people didn't have fully functioning brains.

"What do you get out of those women?" she asked Lenny, staring over at him from her chair in the living room.

He jabbed guiltily at his screen from his flat-out position on the sofa and looked at her. "What bloody women?"

"The ones you ogle on your phone."

"Dunno what you're on about."

Of course you bloody do. "I am interested to know why you do it. I am fascinated by the acts of humans." She shrugged.

He shrugged, too. "Does it upset you?"

She thought about how he played with himself as if she wasn't there. While she didn't care what he did in her absence, it was his inconsideration that annoyed her the most. "You can look, but to flaunt it in front of me is very rude. I do not like rude people, you know this."

"I'll do it when you're out or asleep then."

"Hmm." She'd put up with it until she could get rid of him. But first... "Where are we going on holiday? Do not think you can get away with dangling a carrot and not letting me eat it."

He smiled at that. "Ten days in Corfu, already booked. The Caribbean was too dear. We ought to make ourselves scarce for a bit."

"It is a good job that fits in nicely with my plans," she said. "God forbid you ever check things with me first. I will have to tell Zac he needs to collect his money while we are gone. Then I have work when we get back. I would like you to help me."

"Really? That's just the best."

No, the act of strangling you afterwards, that is the best.

CHAPTER NINETEEN

Paperwork complete, info transferred from Mike's notebook to the whiteboard, for Bethany, the morning had zipped by. She'd fitted in a power nap around seven a.m., as had Mike. They'd kipped in their chairs, feet up on Fran's and Leona's, uncomfortable, but better than dragging their arses all day. There was something to be said about fifty minutes of sleep—she felt like she'd fully caught up, although later, she'd flag again, but she'd deal with that when she had to.

Fran and Leona were still digging about—Fran on social media, Leona on the victims' pasts. Clancy's squat address had been found, so that was something positive. Bethany and Mike were on their way there in a sec to see if anyone was in and could tell them snippets about Clancy that would lead to the killer. Talitia had tucked herself away in the corner, checking CCTV again so they had a third pair of eyes on it—Christ, Bethany wanted the black and red cars found. Glen currently tacked a map to a corkboard so he could stick pins in all the body dump locations. It was obvious the killer either lived on the estate the library was on, or they didn't and had chosen it on purpose because it wasn't near their home.

"Okay, we're nipping out now," Bethany said. "See you in a bit."

She drove towards the squat, chatting to Mike about some show he'd finished watching the other night. The usual weirdo murderers. He'd just got to the bit where someone had been crammed into an oil drum, naked, and she stopped him, hand raised.

"What the fuck is going on there?" She pointed ahead while pulling over at their destination.

"Looks like they're having a street party."

People danced barefoot on the pavement, their clothing showing how far they'd sunk in the pool of life. Some filthy, some ragged, and others were downright drowning. No one's hair had seen water for a while, and yellow-tinged skin on a couple of them indicated jaundice, their livers probably fucked from booze. All eleven people needed a good meal, their bodies stick-thin, waving arms riddled with puncture wounds and bruises on the inner elbows.

"Druggies if you ask me," Mike said.

"We'll need to be careful. We're not going inside that house. Too much of a risk being stuck with dirty needles. I'll handle this, I've got an idea—and you can call me insane afterwards. Follow my lead."

They got out and approached the gyrating group, the strains of Shaggy's *It Wasn't Me* wafting out through the open doorway. Thankfully, it was low, so they'd be able to hear themselves speak.

"Can you help me?" Bethany asked, twitching a bit, acting jittery, some woman who was after a fix. "I need Clancy. Like, you know, *need* her."

Two people stared, a man and a woman, obviously not as high as the others. The man squinted, beer bottle halfway to his slack mouth. He sniffed.

"What d'you want her for?" he said.

Bethany glanced up and down the street, furtive, fake-worried. "Do I have to spell it out?" she hissed. "She didn't meet me like she was supposed to. I need what she can give me. Where is she, for God's sake? I'm on my way down and need to go up again, do you get me?"

He nodded. "She can't get you what you want. She's dead."

"What?" Bethany hoped her shriek wasn't over the top. "But I need my shit! I bet it was that fucker in the black car." She nodded. "Clancy told me about him."

"Doubt it," the woman said, stringy brown hair all but dripping with grease. "It'll be that fucking Animal Gang."

What the hell is that? "Gang? So we need to worry about *those* now?" Bethany sighed. "You tell me who they are, and I'll bloody sort them. No one stops me getting my gear. God, I'm desperate. It's starting to hurt..." She slapped a hand on her stomach.

Greasy Hair narrowed her eyes. "You don't look the type."

"Believe me," Mike said, "she's the type. I'm her brother, so I should know. If she doesn't get something soon, she's going to be a wreck. This"— he gestured to Bethany's appearance—"won't be like it for long. She slashes at her clothes and all sorts."

"Weird," Greasy Hair muttered.

"The Animal Gang is a few kids Clancy used to hang round with," the man said, as though Mike hadn't spoken. "When she was a kid. They robbed—"

Greasy Hair slapped his arm. "Shut up."

"What? She's fucking snuffed it! They can't hurt her now, can they. That gang have a lot to answer for, especially the ringleader."

Shaggy insisted it wasn't him.

"I'm not saying a word." Greasy Hair danced off to join the others.

"Look," Bethany said. "I'll go and find these animal fuckers. Sort them."

"Thanks. Clancy would like that." The man grinned, displaying alarming brown teeth. "I don't know who they are, just that they robbed the Stellar shop years ago. That's what Clancy said anyway. Some old dear recognised Clancy's voice, and she'd been worried ever since that one of the Animals would come after her for the hassle she'd caused."

"How do you know this then?" Bethany asked, twitching again.

"Clancy told us one night when she was smacked off her tits."

"I need more info. I can't go and sort these people based on what you've told me. I know someone who will do them right over, but they need deets."

He sighed. "She said the old dear was killed after the robbery, so was some woman and her kids. Something about a house fire. Stellar was the only other one who knew she'd been in the shop, so she shagged him for a few years to pay him off. Like I said, I don't know these people. I didn't grow up here. Now, can I go back to the party? It's a celebration of Clancy's life. She'd want us to do this."

"Shit. Where am I meant to get my gear from now? Oi, you lot." She pointed at the others. "What's this about the Animal Gang?"

They ignored her. Chaka Demus and Pliers shoved Shaggy out of the way and sang about wanting to be teased. Clancy's friends carried on dancing.

Fat lot of good they are. Too doped up to know what I'm talking about.

Bethany stormed off and got in the car. With Mike beside her, the doors closed, their seat belts on, she said, "What the bloody hell has been going on?" She drove off, parking around the corner. "I have to ring Fran." She jabbed at her phone. "Hi, it's me. I need one of you to look into a robbery a few years back at Stellar's shop. A gang of kids. Then I need details of an old lady being killed around the same time, and a house fire where a woman and her children died." *Shit, had Vinny attended?* "That's all I could get out of two people at the squat. The others were...in no state to speak to us, shall we say. Ring the fire station as well. Ask for a man called Cuppa—he was Vinny's mate. He might remember that fire."

"Okay," Fran said. "Stellar could have been robbed a few times, so we'll sift through and see which ones involved a gang."

"The Animal Gang, apparently."

"Lovely. Wonder where they come up with these names?"

"No idea. I'm just—" She closed her eyes for a second to calm herself. Seemed the power nap hadn't quite sanded the edges off her nerves like she'd thought. "Hang on, I've got another call. Speak later." She switched over. "Hello?"

"Rob," he said.

"And the day is going to take a nosedive, yes?"

"Afraid so. Four this time."

"Um, I beg your pardon?"

"Four. All yours. Same ticks and whatnot. Found by a council worker."

She actually wanted to cry. "Okay, where?"

He gave the location.

"Right, on our way." She put her phone on her lap. Glanced at Mike. "Four more. Down by the river."

"*How* many?"

"I know. Just give me a sec." She rang DI Tracy Collier from Serious Crimes.

"What do you bloody want?" Tracy said in her usual acerbic way.

"Not you." Bethany laughed. "Just checking in. I've had four bodies turn up, now another four, same killer. You might well get a phone call from Kribbs to come and help. Fair warning."

"Shit. All right. Let's hope no news is good news. Or even better, you solve it so I don't have to come and poke my nose in. Want to talk about it?"

"Not yet. Might bend your ear if the connection between them all doesn't show itself soon."

"Fab." Deadpan. "Will look forward to it." Sarcasm.

"No, you won't."

"True. Bugger off then. I've got stuff to do."

"Hopefully we won't speak soon." Bethany slid her phone in her pocket and drove away. "She's a bundle of non-fun, that one. Can't help but like her, though."

"I was thinking while you were on the phone. If our killer didn't do Ian and Jambrea, and we have two people to look for, how have four been done at once? Tag team? Two each?"

She turned onto the main road that led to the river. "Maybe the gun is enough of a threat."

"Hmm, but to be able to kill one while three are just, what, standing there?"

"Unless they were done one at a time and taken to the river afterwards. We're going over the same kind of supposition as we did with the Mintwell buildings bodies. The scene will tell the story—or some of it anyway. Ah, it's just along here." She sped over a large expanse of grass, heading for a council lorry, a SOCO van, and a patrol car. Stopping behind them, she got out and viewed the scene.

A tent had been erected, one of the larger ones. Several SOCO were busy in the surrounding area. The river burbled beyond, cackling over rocks that poked through the surface, and over the other side, trees stood in a line, conifers, bushy enough to hide what the killer was doing. She turned to look the other way, from where they'd come. An empty road, miles of fields stretching off into the distance ahead and to the right, Shadwell's outskirts to the left. The area was isolated, an easy murder playground. However, as she swivelled to

Shadwell, she acknowledged just how close it was past the conifers. A walk away, maybe half a mile. The river tapered the nearer it got to the buildings, then curved so some outlying homes had a nice view of it from the bottom of their back gardens. Could someone have seen the murders if looking out of a bedroom window?

She got her phone out.

Bethany: FRAN, FOUR MORE BODIES.

She told her the location and asked for Talitia and Glen to come out and do house-to-house.

Fran: FOUR? WHAT IS *WRONG* WITH THIS PERSON?

Bethany: GOD KNOWS. CCTV, PLEASE. IT'S DOUBTFUL ANYTHING WAS CAUGHT ON IT, BUT YOU NEVER KNOW. GOT TO GO.

She walked with Mike to the SOCO van, and they got dressed then signed the log with Nicola Eccles.

"The man who found them is in his lorry." Nicola nodded that way. "A William Voltra."

"Right, we'll have a quick chat with him now."

Bethany and Mike approached the lorry, the kind with a flat bed and wire mesh sides, filled halfway with branches and various bits of foliage. Some black bags were piled at the back, grass cuttings peering out through gaps where he hadn't quiet tied the handles properly. She unzipped her suit and produced her ID, showing it to him through his side window. He opened the door and climbed out, face ashen, hands shaking. Around fifty or so, with greying hair at the temples, he gave them a wobbly smile.

"William Voltra?" she asked, slipping her ID away and drawing up her zip.

He nodded. "I just... I was... It wasn't..."

"Take a deep breath," she said. "It's easier if I ask questions and you answer, okay? Let's start from the beginning. What are you doing here?"

"I'm meant to be cutting the shrubbery all along the river. My mate's coming in a bit with the ride-on mower."

"He'll obviously need to stay away. Can you ring him quickly?" She waited while he did that, then, "So what did you do when you arrived?"

"Well, I'd normally start down closer to Shadwell but decided to drive this stretch to see how much work needed doing, you know, get myself psyched up for it. So I came along the road there and spotted some humps. Thought it was people having a lie down after a picnic at first—that's not unheard of here. They feed the ducks and whatever. Couple of swans, but they're a bit mardy and can get the hump. Anyway, I left the road, parked right here. Then I walked over, because something didn't feel right. The closer I got, the worse the feeling was, and then..." He swallowed. "And then I saw the blood on one of the foreheads, registered the carving, and I copped an eyeful of his foot. The toe...God, the toe was missing, and I knew it was to do with them murders in the paper."

Bethany had sympathy for him. Out here to do a job, and he finds that. "How close to the bodies were you?"

"About three metres away. Didn't go any closer, I just rang the police. Miss Eccles, I think that's her name, she got here within two minutes, and she rang in to call off the ambulance, because the nine-nine-nine woman was sending one out. I stood here until Miss Eccles arrived, spoke to her after she'd gone to check if anyone was alive, then I got in my lorry and waited."

"Okay, we'll need a proper statement, so if you can get down to the station later or early tomorrow, that would be great. We need to go in the tent now, and you can leave. Are you all right to drive?"

"Yeah. I just want to get away from here, to be honest."

"I'm sure you do." She smiled and waited for him to reverse. "Poor sod."

"It's got to be awful, hasn't it." Mike shook his head. "Let's go and see what's going on then."

They walked to the tent, and Bethany pulled the flap back, going inside first. Isabelle greeted them in her usual happy way, and this time, Bethany ripped the plaster off and looked at the bodies immediately.

"Oh," she said and stared at Mike.

"Interesting." He raised his eyebrows.

"Don't keep me in suspenders," Isabelle said. "Share? Because I'm buggered if I know what that means." She pointed to the four men on the

255

ground, placed in a straight line, side by side in height order.

Writing on their foreheads tied in with what the man at the squat had told them. The wording, in capitals, had been penned along the inner length of the tick: I'M AN ANIMAL.

Bethany explained about the Stellar robbery. "So these men could be the gang members."

"Okay." Isabelle frowned. "These four, plus Clancy and Ian Stellar, are all connected, but what about Susan Burrow, Keith Crow, Bert Yawling, and Jambrea Gaff? That's ten victims, more than the nine needed for the grid."

"It's bound to become clear soon." Bethany gave the bodies her attention again. Everything was in place: tick, tack, toe. Blood coated the grass beneath their feet, so they'd been killed here. She inspected their temples. "No gun imprints on any of them."

Mike moved to look as well. "So how the hell did the killer get them to comply?"

"I'm at a loss." Bethany shook her head. "Any ID?"

"Yes." Isabelle gave their names for Mike to write down.

"I'll just message them to Fran," he said.

Bethany sighed, glad he'd taken over that job. Their afternoon was going to be filled with visits to the next of kins, hoping that a glimmer of information sparkled so they'd be able to work out who connected all these people.

"Did you notice their feet, the bare ones?" Isabelle asked.

Bethany had a gander at the one closest to her. MY NAME IS PIG had been scrawled on it in blue biro. She stepped along. They all had the same, except the animals were different. Cow, Donkey, Sheep. "I wonder what Clancy's name was?"

Mike had finished messaging. "And, is the killer another gang member? Were they *all* in the gang?"

Isabelle laughed. "What, even Bert Yawling? Who'd want an old bloke?"

Mike shrugged. "Then maybe some were members and the others knew about them. One or two people decided they needed to silence them for whatever reason."

"That's easily checked in Jambrea's case," Bethany said. "Ring her mum, will you?"

Mike walked out of the tent.

Bethany's phone bleeped.

Fran: ARMED ROBBERY FIFTEEN YEARS AGO BY A GROUP OF KIDS. WEIRD STUFF: THEY WENT IN WITH ANIMAL MASKS ON.

Bethany's heart skipped a beat.

Bethany: DOES THE REPORT SAY WHAT THEY ARE?

Fran: PIG, DONKEY, SHEEP, COW, GORILLA, AND CHICKEN.

Bethany: WELL, WE HAVE FOUR OF THOSE HERE NOW. EXPLAIN LATER. HERE ARE THEIR NAMES.

She typed them out.

Fran: CHEERS. GET THIS. KEITH CROW WAS THERE. HE MADE A STATEMENT.

Bethany: BLOODY HELL!

Fran: HE SAID HE STOPPED ONE OF THEM, THE GORILLA, AS THEY WERE LEGGING IT OUT OF THE SHOP, BUT THE GORILLA GOT AWAY. WANT ME TO GET HOLD OF EVAN CROW AND SEE IF HE REMEMBERS ANYTHING? I'LL SEARCH FOR THE OLD LADY DEATH AND THE FIRE AFTERWARDS. I'LL PUT LEONA ON NEXT OF KIN FOR THOSE PEOPLE PLUS THE BODIES YOU'VE GOT THERE.

Bethany: OKAY. LET ME KNOW AS SOON AS YOU HAVE ANYTHING USEFUL FROM EVAN.

Mike came back in. "Mrs Gaff doesn't know anything about a gang."

"Doesn't matter." She told him about Fran's message. "So who are Chicken and Gorilla?"

"Clancy and...?"

"Find that out, and I think we have our killer."

CHAPTER TWENTY

Hours had passed since a car had rumbled down the track beside the allotment. At the time, Dave Quantock had climbed on top of an old orange box and poked his head over the hedge, thinking the police had come back for whatever reason, but a black Golf had turned at the end, going towards the copse. Dave had lost himself in weeding Bert Yawling's patch then, not in memory of the pervert, but for the sake of whoever took it over next. It'd be a shame to let it go to ruin.

Now, with his own lettuces and a couple of onions pulled up for dinner—he wouldn't steal Bert's, Dave wasn't that kind of man—he stretched his back. Time had curved his spine in that cruel way it had, swelling his knuckles, too, while it was at it. That was why he took so long to work on his patch. Creaks and aches held him back.

He frowned. Thought about that Golf. Maybe the driver had taken a sneaky shortcut across the field to the estate. Still, it wouldn't hurt to check on his way home, would it.

Veg in a black mesh bag, he waved at the others tending to their crops and left via the gate. The walk up the track took a while—his knee joints protested—and he came out at the end, sighing at having to tromp over the field. Maybe he ought to come here in the car sometimes, give his body a rest.

He glanced left and shivered at the police tape hanging from a distant tree trunk. It bothered him, it being left there, so he went that way with the intent to remove it. The city was littered enough as it was, and some bird might tug at it for a nest and end up choking. You just didn't know, did you.

A couple of minutes later, Dave snipped the tape with a pair of cutters he still had in his pocket from when he'd used them for the wire to wrap round his runner bean stems. They'd seemed to climb higher overnight, the tops bending over, waggling.

He glanced into the copse, curious about what other mess had been left behind from the police. His conscience wouldn't let him rest, so he traipsed in there, looking around as he walked. Ahead, a child's bike lay on its side, and he recognised it as the one belonging to Kitty Longshaw, that cute nipper who lived in his street. She was always coming here to play, and he'd mentioned to her mother once that the world wasn't the same as it used to be, and four-year-old kiddies just couldn't go out by themselves like Kitty did. He'd received a *Fuck off, knobend* for his trouble, and wasn't that just charming.

He frowned. "Kitty?"

She'd be behind one of the trees, he'd bet, ready to leap out at him, laughing if he jumped a mile in pretend fright.

"Come on, love, you shouldn't be in here. Best you go home, eh? I'll take you, make sure you get back safe. It's Mr Quantock. You know me."

No answer, save for a bird twittering.

Dave moved on, checking each tree, but they were birches and too thin anyway. She'd be easily seen. He picked a stout oak and stepped towards it, his stomach churning. Something wasn't right, he felt it in his warped old bones. The hairs on the back of his neck stood on end.

Another step. Another.

And there she was, that little girl, on her back, the copse ground her bed. A tick and blood wrecked her forehead above widened eyes, those eyes the colour of the Mediterranean Sea with a kiss of frost. Her T-shirt had been pushed up, her belly revealed, gold discs on it, and a tiny toe stuck out of her navel.

Dave staggered backwards, pain streaking across his chest, and his eyes burned, fizzing his vision. A strangled sob wrenched out of him, and he dropped to his knees, fumbling in his pocket for his phone. He'd programmed that detective's number in it, and after a few failed attempts, managed to bring up his contact list.

I told your mummy. I told her you shouldn't be out alone. You poor sweet angel...

CHAPTER TWENTY-ONE

Presley had arrived and had done his usual. He stood from crouching beside the fourth body and looked skywards, obviously working something out. He lowered his head. "Going by the temps, and this is a rough estimate because they were killed so close together—"

Bethany's phone ringing stopped him continuing.

"Two seconds." She didn't recognise the number on the screen and frowned. It could be anyone she'd given her business card to in the past.

"Detective Smith?" a man said. Out of breath. Gasping.

"Yes, are you all right, sir?"

"No. This is just awful. It's Kitty Longshaw. She's... She's been killed by that bloody bastard."

Is that Dave Quantock?

Bethany's legs went a tad limp. "Who is Kitty?"

"She's...she's a little girl in my street. Four. Only four!"

A lump rose in Bethany's throat, and she felt sick. Her pulse thudded wildly. "A *child*?" Cold drenched her skin, then it went clammy.

"Yes, come quickly. I can't stand to be here. She's... Her forehead. Her tiny toe..."

Oh no. No.

Murderous anger surged, and, not for the first time, Bethany understood exactly how some people could kill. If she got her hands on who they were after right this minute, she'd go for them, fucking beat the shit out of them. *Calm down. Concentrate.* "Where are you?"

"The copse. By the allotment. Where Bert was. *Exactly there.*"

Bloody hell, that was bold. The police presence hadn't been gone that long. "Okay, stay where you are. We're coming now." She ended the call and rang Rob, her hands shaking. "Get me a couple of uniforms back down the copse. A kiddie's been killed. Kitty Longshaw. Get Alice Jacobs round to her mother, now!"

"Oh, dear God..."

She shoved her phone away. "Mike, Isabelle, we have to go. The copse behind the allotment. A four-year-old, for Pete's sake..."

Bethany bolted out of the tent, grabbing a few pairs of booties and gloves from the box by the flap so they could put them on at the copse. She jumped in her car, gunning the engine as Mike crashed onto his seat. Heart hurting, eyes stinging, she held back the tears and the need to scream, belting along the road and into Shadwell, thankful Mike hadn't started a conversation she wasn't capable of holding at the moment. A girl. Someone so innocent. What was this monster playing at? Why would a kid be any threat to them?

She sped adjacent to the allotment then careened onto the track, speeding down it and taking a too-fast turn out onto the field. She struggled with controlling the steering, panicking the car would tumble over, but it continued on with her solid grip on the wheel. At the copse, she stopped and slid fresh booties and gloves on, Mike doing the same. A set for Dave clutched in her hand, she ran through the trees, her breathing heavy, her body exactly the same. There he was, on his knees, sobbing, a broken man. His hands covered his face, knuckles big and gnarly.

"Deal with him," she said to Mike, handing over the protectives.

She walked forward, to the body of a precious munchkin who'd had all the vibrancy and life taken out of her by a sick bastard intent on wrecking so many lives.

"Why you, darling?" she whispered, and God, the tears came then, hot and streaming, her cheeks wet, the lump in her throat too big to swallow.

To see a tick on such a small forehead was more hideous than it had been with the adults, and that dinky toe...it was barely visible in her innie, just the tip and the nail on show—a nail painted in sparkly pink polish. Her bare foot, streaked with blood, had once had a sock on it and a pretty sandal like the other one, but those things had been left on the ground, discarded, much like Kitty.

This time, the tacks formed a pattern. A picture.

An eye.

What did that mean? Had the killer been watching her, was that it?

She faced Mike. Dave stood now, Mike's arm around his back, and Dave leant on him to put the booties on. She went to him, helped him out, and remained quiet while he pulled the gloves on and stared down at them as if he couldn't believe they covered his hands.

And he told her then, how the black car had gone past, how he'd come to find Kitty, how he'd warned her mother, Carla Longshaw, about the girl being out alone at such a young age. His description of Carla left a lot to be desired—she liked drinking, smoking, and pretending she wasn't a mum. Kitty's dad wasn't in the picture, and the only reason Kitty had clean clothes was because her nan popped round every evening, where she made sure she was fed and bathed.

Isabelle and one of her other teams arrived, so Bethany and Mike led Dave out of the copse. At Bethany's car, they took off their protective clothing, put it in the boot, then walked across the field to Dave's street.

"She lives there, the mother," Dave said, his voice hoarse. He pointed to a red door. "I don't think I'll be able to look at her again after this. It was bad enough before...before..."

"I know exactly how you feel." Bethany patted him.

He ambled away, and she made sure he'd gone through his front door with the assurance that someone would be out to interview him properly, then she turned to Mike.

"You deal with her. I can't. I'm likely to lose it." She jerked her head at Miss Longshaw's door. "I'm ready to commit murder here, which is ironic, considering."

They shuffled up the path, Bethany sluggish after the adrenaline rush and the awful shock of seeing a dead child. She'd remember it for as long as she lived. That ponytail askew. Her button nose. Rosebud mouth. Those startled eyes that showed how terrified she'd been.

Stop it.

Mike knocked and took his ID out. "You okay?"

She shook her head. "Did you see her, that poor baby?" she whispered.

"I didn't...I didn't look on purpose." He let out a ragged breath. "God. I can't cry on the job, but..."

"I know." She linked her pinky finger with his briefly. "Hold it together. Until we're done here."

A twenty-something woman answered, all grey velour tracksuit, a cigarette in one hand, a glass in the other.

Alice Jacobs couldn't have arrived yet, otherwise she'd be the one standing there. Bethany had forgotten to check the street for her car.

"Carla Longshaw?" Mike held his identification up. "I'm DS Mike Wilkins, and this is DI Bethany Smith. We need to come in."

"Ah, I saw you with old Quantock. Got hold of you about Kitty, has he? She plays out on her bike after morning nursery. Big deal."

It is a big deal, you stupid, arrogant bitch.

"Is she home now?" he asked, probably because the only means of identification they had was from Dave, and they couldn't assume.

"Come to think of it, no." She took a swig from her glass.

"What colour is her bike?" he asked.

"Pink and white."

"What is she wearing today?"

"Dunno. She'll have her sandals on, though. Got no other shoes. She took her uniform off and dressed herself after nursery and went straight out."

"Inside, please, Miss Longshaw." Mike put his foot on the step.

"No, whatever you've got to say can be said out here."

"What we have to say has to be said indoors. Come on." Mike took her elbow and guided her inside.

She protested all the while, and, closing the door, Bethany took a moment to compose herself. What had Kitty's life been like within these walls? Had she loved her mother despite the way she was? Did she long for nighttime when Nanny came round to fill her belly with good food and give her cuddles? Had Nanny painted her tiny nails with that sparkly polish? Was Carla so interested in herself and what she wanted that Kitty's needs had been at the bottom of the list?

She imagined that little girl pedalling away on her bike, happy, carefree for the minutes and hours she wasn't at home.

Mike's voice droned quietly.

A person-shaped shadow on the wall had Bethany turning. She opened the door. Alice was here, standing there with tears in her eyes. A child's death always hit everyone hard. She came in.

Bethany gestured for her to go into the living room, whispering, "I can't. I've got nothing left."

Alice nodded and disappeared inside. A minute or so passed.

A scream came then, and Bethany held her breath, scrunched her eyes shut, and couldn't for the life of her swallow the lump in her throat. The scream ended as quickly as it had begun.

Then Carla said, "That's all I need, a bloody funeral to find the money for."

Unable to stand being in this hateful house any longer, Bethany walked out to the car. Leant against it and stared at the sky, wondering if Kitty had got to Heaven yet and was gazing down. "Look after her, Vin, until I get there." Then she sobbed, head bent, uncaring whether anyone saw her. She cried for that kid, for all the victims, their families, and also for herself.

"Detective Smith?"

She wiped her face and rounded the car, meeting Dave in the middle of the road. He'd had another good cry, too, going by his blotchy face. His wife stood at their gate, wringing her hands.

"I remembered something," he said.

Mike strode across from Carla's, probably glad to leave that cow in Alice's hands. He joined them

"Go on..." Bethany said to Dave.

"The black car. It was a Golf."

Mike sucked in a breath.

"What's the matter?" Bethany asked him.

"We need to go," he said. "Now."

"Sorry to rush off, Dave, and thank you." Bethany slid into the driver's seat. With Mike belted up, too, she said, "What the hell is going on?" *Can I take any more today?*

"Black Golf. There was one outside Jambrea Gaff's place. Get a move on. I'll ring Rob now to do a check."

"What? You think this is *Ferguson*? Shit!"

She shot off, and Mike rang the front desk, selecting speakerphone.

"It's Mike. We need a car check for a Zac Ferguson." He gave the address.

The wait for an answer seemed to take ages, but it was probably only a minute or so.

"Golf GTI, black, registered to him," Rob said.

"Cheers." Mike ended the call. "If it isn't him, we still want to know whether he drove down that track today."

Bethany's phone rang. "Fuck it. Get that, will you?" She handed it over.

Mike answered. "Hang on. I need to put it on speaker." He swiped the screen. "Go on, Fran."

"Leona's been looking at CCTV, the roads prior to, as well as leading to the river. She spotted a dark vehicle, but the number plate's dirty. It headed out of Shadwell, past that little row of shops on the outskirts on the main road. Shortly afterwards, an SUV comes along, and that's registered to James Pinkerton, one of those deceased at the river. From what we could see, there were four people in it, although they're just shapes really. Later, the dark car comes past again, and the driver stops at the shop. I've phoned them, and they've looked at their internal footage. It was a man, and he bought a bottle of vodka." She gave them a description that matched Zac's.

"Right, we're on our way to his place now. We'll wait for uniform backup," Bethany said, slowing a bit. "Can you get Talitia and Glen off house-to-house by the river and over to Ferguson's, please? Tell them to park out of sight. Thanks. We need to go, so catch you later."

Then she drove to Ferguson's street, nudging her car between two others a few doors down. The Golf sat at the kerb, the number plate dirty, thick with mud, as though he'd deliberately obscured it. While they had no proof whatsoever Zac was their man, apart from Dave Quantock's sighting of the Golf, plus what was on CCTV, they had to follow all leads.

While they sat waiting, she thought about her interactions with him. He'd been distraught at his girlfriend's death, and that was where the confusion came in.

"Do you reckon he killed Jambrea?" she asked. "Think about how he behaved after we visited him. He was genuinely gutted."

"Maybe he killed everyone else, and the other person who was at Mintwell killed her. It makes sense two people were involved because of the tacks being taken out of Clancy's stomach. If he'd planned to kill all three, he'd have shared the drawing pins between them. Instead, it's like someone else came along and took them out so their murders mimicked his."

"A good way to hide what you've done, blaming him," she said. "So we're looking at someone else entirely for Jambrea and Ian. Is it just a massive coincidence the killers both went to the same place to commit their crimes? That is just creepy."

"How are we going to play this?" Mike asked.

"We're here to check on how he is after the death of his girlfriend, and I have a few other things up my sleeve. I'm going to tell a lot of lies but make out the lies are just our thoughts, not fact. It could make him panic and trip up."

"He's going to think it weird that uniforms are with us."

"We'll do what we've done in the past," she said. "Leave the front door ajar, then Talitia and Glen can come in if they hear things getting out of hand. Here they are now, look."

The patrol car stopped up the road, and Bethany drove there and parked behind it. They chatted about the game plan, ensuring everyone knew where they stood in the upcoming interaction.

If he was the one who'd killed Kitty Longshaw, Bethany didn't know if she'd be able to keep her hands off him, but she'd have to play it cool, push her personal feelings aside. The job came first, always.

CHAPTER TWENTY-TWO

Zac lounged on the sofa, thinking about the day. The telly was on, a voice babbling out of it, low where he had the sound turned down. Had he made a mistake in killing that kid? The police would be all over that, more so than the adult deaths, and the public would have a right old mare. Shadwell would hit the national news, the whole country going into mourning.

Great way to get the spotlight on him as being the boyfriend of one of the victims.

Fuck it.

Something had come over him, though, this massive need to be rid of that kid so she didn't open her mouth and get him in the shit. Now, because of what he'd done, he'd probably be in the shit anyway. There'd be too many probing eyes coming into Shadwell, journalists who could spot a wrongun as soon as look at them. He'd have to stay under the radar, make out he was grieving for Jambrea in peace. There was a bloke, a school caretaker, Zac couldn't remember his name, who'd killed two girls. He'd been caught based on how he'd behaved when speaking to the press. Zac wouldn't make that mistake.

But that child. A *child*. What was he playing at? She was so small, fragile, and his fingers had overlapped at the back of her neck when he'd…

Guilt prodded him, even though he'd had to do it, had to add her to the grid. Yet at the same time, he deserved to live without the people he'd murdered bugging him, and the child had bugged him, too, so it was her fault, what he'd done. If she hadn't been at the copse the first time, she'd still be alive, wouldn't she, belting it around on that fucking bike of hers.

Had she been found yet? If she hadn't, surely her mother would have phoned the police by now, saying she hadn't come home. They'd be searching for her, and someone would stumble on her in the copse. If they didn't, those search dogs would sniff her out, no problem.

But there was a bright side. The grid boxes were all filled with *his* crosses, no one else's, and that counted for something, didn't it? Didn't matter that the last box was a randomer. All right, she wasn't so random, not really, but whatever.

He switched the telly off. No point in having it on. He wasn't watching it, too caught up in getting to grips with the fact it was all over. Done. He'd set out to—

Someone knocked on the door.

Shit, if that was Jambrea's mum, coming round here to collect her stuff... He didn't want to see the old bag. She'd give him an earful, and he just wasn't in the mood.

He got up, sighing, telling himself to deal with her, let her in, then that would be the end of his association with her, apart from the funeral. And that'd be weird, wouldn't it, because he'd envisaged how he'd behave at it, back when he'd been planning and thought *he'd* be the one to kill her. Now, she was someone else's prize, but he supposed he could still cry. Tears of anger, but no one else would know that, would they.

In the hallway, he frowned at the shape of two people out on the step. So she'd brought a friend, a witness, in case he gave her hassle. He was too worn out to care. It'd probably be her neighbour with her, the one with the wonky eye that leaked all the time.

He swung the door open, ready to be polite, and got the shock of his life. Those coppers stood there, the ones who'd come to tell him Jambrea was dead. Composing his face into an expression of relief, of being glad they were here, he sighed. They must be checking to see if he was all right, or maybe they'd found out who'd killed her and were about to tell him. It'd be handy if that person got the blame for all Zac's work. He wouldn't have to look over his shoulder then.

"Hello," he said, stepping back so they could come in. "Would you like a cuppa?" They'd had one before, so it stood to reason they'd want one again. Visitors always did.

"How are you, Zac?" Smith said.

"Just about coping." He gave a sad smile.

"You poor thing." She smiled back. "No, no, don't you worry about the door. Mike will sort that." She took his arm and guided him to the kitchen. "Have a sit down. I'll make you a drink. You must be exhausted, all that grief."

It was weird seeing her touch his kettle, doing something Jambrea normally did. It was nice to have a woman here again. Maybe he'd meet someone new soon. That'd be great.

'Come here, Zac, and make me a cup of tea.'

Anxiety spiking, he blinked that voice away and did as Smith had said, plonking his arse at the table. "Yeah, grief, it's a weird old thing, isn't it. All right one minute, upset the next." Although he wasn't referring to grief, just the anger that came in large doses when he wasn't expecting it. Mind

278

you, he'd lived with it for so long, he should be used to it by now. Sometimes, it got him so he panicked and didn't know what to say or do. He'd have to get a grip on it until the coppers had gone. Couldn't afford to mess up. "I keep thinking she's going to walk in any minute." That was true. Walk in and have a go at him. Ask him for those fake tits again. Or some more Jimmy's. Demanding cow.

A knot tightened in his stomach. He couldn't think about Jambrea anymore.

"Yes, I lost my husband, so I understand where you're coming from." Smith poked about finding a cup and teaspoon.

That Wilkins fella, he stood blocking the doorway. He seemed a bit annoyed, on edge.

"Any news on who did it?" Zac needed to know the score.

She spooned sugar in the cup. "There have been more murders. It's awful, don't you think?"

No, but you wouldn't understand. They deserved it. All of them. "Blimey. What's the world coming to?" *That's what people say. She'll think I'm just a normal bloke, no one to worry about.*

"Since Jambrea, there have been five bodies." She poured water into the cup. Steam puffed up. "Four of them were men who used to belong to a gang when they were teenagers."

His stomach clenched, the knot giving him gyp. A lot of gyp. Shit. If they knew that, someone might open their mouth and say *he'd* been a member an' all. *And* that Clancy was. How did they know it was a gang? He'd only written cryptic messages on the bodies. "A gang?"

"Yes, the Animal Gang. They'd have formed when you were in your teens. Heard of them?" She finished squeezing his teabag then added milk. Stirred.

He didn't answer. She handed him his drink.

"Cheers. You two not having one?" he asked.

"No, we're not stopping long. We've got a suspect to take down the station. Anyway, back to what I was saying. We have reason to believe that gang robbed Mr Stellar's shop years ago, and that's a bit chilling, because he's one of the deceased. And Clancy Robins, she was in the gang, too."

Fuck. They'd really done their homework. He sipped his tea, pleased his hand didn't shake. She'd made it well nice, just the way he liked it.

"And we're guessing here," she went on, "but Keith Crow, another of the victims, he gave a statement after the robbery, so it's looking likely that with all the gang members dead, plus Mr Stellar and Keith..." She rubbed her forehead. "You can well imagine we've put two and two together."

And come up with what?

"Now, we also know Bert Yawling was a pervert, and whoever killed him did so because of sexual abuse."

How do they know these things? I didn't tell anyone what he did to me.

She shook her head. "So sad for the children he messed around with. We feel sorry for them, don't we, Mike?"

280

Wilkins nodded. "Bert's been at it for years. That lad we spoke to, Bert's latest... Terrible."

So Bert *had* still been doing what he shouldn't. Zac had been right about that. Killing him had definitely been for the best.

Smith leant against the worktop and folded her arms. "We shouldn't even be talking to you about it."

But I need you to. "It's all right. Not like I'm going to be telling anyone, is it."

"Okay. A four-year-old girl was also killed. Kitty Longshaw. We've been doing a bit of thinking, and we reckon the killer was touched up by Mr Yawling, and they went weird in the head and started doing the same to Kitty."

No. Fucking hell no. That's not right. He gripped the cup, ignoring the heat seeping into his skin.

"So she was going to tell on him, and he ended up having to kill her. Thing is, we think Susan Burrow knew all about it, and she told Jambrea when she came into the library. A witness probably heard the conversation. What a mess, eh?"

Zac nodded. *But Jambrea didn't go to the library. She didn't even know that bloody Burrow woman. Did she?* "Sounds a right old pickle."

"Hmm. The best bit is, someone's told us they saw a black car going down the side of the allotment today, round the back where Bert and Kitty were killed. Won't be long before we pick up the number plate from the camera. Just before we came here, we received news that there's one at

281

the allotment—a camera, I mean. The council put it up to catch people nicking all the veg." She tucked a strand of hair behind her ear. "Who'd be rude enough to climb over the gate and pinch lettuce and stuff like that? Who'd be rude enough to rob, full stop?"

"Some people—"

"But there's a lot of it about, people thinking they can do what the hell they want. Take that Animal Gang, for instance. They stole money, cigarettes, alcohol, and, get this, we also think they mugged the old lady who was in the shop at the time. Stole her pension. Well, the chicken and the gorilla did anyway."

No, we didn't! We didn't do that at all! Where did that story come from?

"We also suspect the chicken and gorilla killed the old lady as well, plus a woman and her children. House fire for the latter. Petrol-soaked rag trapped in the letterbox and set alight. Those two had better hope we don't find them." She paused. "But the thing is, we're on to them, so it won't be long."

"It wasn't the gorilla," he blurted. *Oh God. What did I just say? Shit!* "I mean, someone would have seen a gorilla, wouldn't they?"

"If they appeared as a gorilla, yes. Could have just done it as people, you know, without the disguise."

He thought of the masks floating down the river after the robbery. Had the other lads bought more, chickens and gorillas, so Zac and Clancy would be blamed if it got out that members of the Animal Gang had offed those people? Kids their age knew who was in that gang, which animal name belonged to which person. Some of them still lived in Shadwell. What if this made the paper and someone stepped forward, saying Zac had been one of them?

Why did I write on their fucking foreheads?
Because you got cocky. You let anger take over.

"You've gone a bit pale," Smith said. "Sorry, I shouldn't be burdening you with all this."

"It's all right. I don't mind." But he did mind now. Didn't want to know their theories anymore. He needed them to go away. Had to get some time to himself so he could think about what to do. Move then change his name? Get Erica to run his business and send him the cash in padded envelopes, recorded delivery?

"Well, I have to ask you, and please don't take offence, but that car I mentioned, it's a black Golf, and we noticed you have one registered in your name. Can you tell us where you've been today?"

He thought of the camera she'd said about at the allotment. Why hadn't he checked if one was there? It was okay when he'd done Bert because he'd come in from a different direction. And it was fine regarding his number plates, he'd dirtied them up, but what if it had captured his face? Were coppers analysing the footage right now? This minute? Would they ring her while she was here and tell her it was him? He had the urge to run, to get out, but Wilkins still stood in the doorway, and bloody hell, Zac didn't feel well.

Panic swirled in his gut, and sweat beaded above his upper lip.

"Time's sort of gone funny since you were here last," he managed. "I don't even know what day it is." That sounded plausible. He hadn't lied and said he'd stayed in or gone out, just that he couldn't remember. He opened his mouth to say more, but a knock rapped on the front door.

Wilkins turned and left the kitchen. Zac shrugged at Smith as if to say: *No idea who that is*. She shrugged back: *No idea either*. At least that was what he thought she'd soundlessly said. Mike's voice rumbled, then came another one. Shit. What was *she* doing here? So much for not contacting each other like this. She hadn't sent him a message asking for a date. Then again, he'd put his phone on silent earlier. Hadn't wanted to deal with people asking him for this or that.

"Zac, tell this man I am allowed in," Erica said, her thick accent travelling into the kitchen. "I brought a casserole. You need to eat."

"Do you know her?" Smith asked Zac.

He shook his head. "Don't recognise the voice." No way he wanted these coppers knowing he was associated with that bloody Orloff woman. He was in enough shit as it was by the sound of it, without adding his money-lending lark into the mix.

He thought of the money upstairs in the safe. The ticks under the bed on the blackboard grid. The fake gun.

"No visitors, please, Mike," Smith called then smiled at Zac.

"There are police in the street," Erica shouted. "They have uniforms on. I hope there is not going to be any trouble."

He heard the threat loud and clear: *Do not mention me, Zac.*

Fuck off. Just go away!

Wilkins said something or other, then returned to stand in the doorway. "She's gone."

"Nice of her to bring food. Did she take it away with her?" Smith glanced at Wilkins' empty hands.

Wilkins nodded.

"So, back to our conversation before the interruption. The Golf," Smith said. "The same car was caught on camera going to the river earlier, then on the way back. The river's where the Animal Gang were murdered. The thing is, you must have gone out today, because the woman at the little shop there swears you went in and bought a bottle of vodka."

Zac's gaze shot to it where it stood on the worktop by the bread bin, and he cursed himself. How the hell could he get out of this?

"The time the car was spotted," Smith said, "ties in with the murders. Are you *sure* you didn't go out and get vodka today? I see you have a bottle."

He wasn't caught yet. He could blag it. Get rid of them for long enough so he could leave Shadwell. "I did buy it, but I can't tell you if it was today or even in that shop. I'm so messed up since Jambrea... Didn't you get the number plate?"

"No, it's dirty." A pause. "Just like yours."

Erica got in her car, annoyed she hadn't been able to give the casserole to Zac. She'd made the snap decision to get rid of him today, before the holiday, and had dumped a load of Lenny's gear in with the gravy. The plan was for Zac to eat it, fall asleep, then she could go from there.

She placed the dish on the back seat, listening to the police officers talking by a hedge.

"Do you think we'll get called in there?" one said.

"Probably. Bethany's good at getting them to admit things."

So they knew Zac was the killer? That had to be it.

Erica smiled, closed the door, and got in the driver's side. She wouldn't need the casserole after all. Zac was obviously going to get arrested, and she could relax, knowing he was locked up for the rest of his life. The problem she had was: *Will he keep his mouth shut about me and what I do?*

It was fine. She'd get to him inside prison.

She had friends there.

Zac didn't know what to say. His brain had seized up. He hadn't envisaged getting caught so hadn't made up any excuses, no cover stories. Too intent on getting the jobs done, that was his problem.

"Zac, I need you to think back to all the dates and times I'm going to give you," Smith said. "I want you to tell me where you were for every one of them."

"Who remembers where they were?" he said. "I told you, my mind isn't right at the minute. I can't think where I was today, let alone for whatever dates you're going on about." His stomach didn't feel right. He needed the loo. "Look, I've got a bad stomach. I just need..."

He got up and approached the door. Wilkins stared at him, then moved aside so Zac could pass. He walked down the hallway towards the toilet, sensing Wilkins' stare on his back. The front door was ajar. Wilkins couldn't have shut it when Erica had knocked.

Adrenaline seeped into his bloodstream, and he lunged for the door and swung it open. Yanked his keys put of his pocket. Legged it outside to his Golf. Someone smacked into him from the side, and he stumbled, holding a hand out in case he fell. He registered a policewoman in uniform, then Wilkins shouting, "Grab him!" Zac went down, landing on his hip, and the sound of a car engine revving drew his gaze upwards. Erica drove past slowly, staring at him, doing a knife-against-the-throat motion.

Shit. Shit!

Wilkins and the copper hefted him to his feet. Zac's legs went weak, and his chest constricted. Skin going cold, sweat popping out on his face, he was turned around so his back pressed on his car.

Smith came towards him. "Why did you run, Zac? Got something to hide, have you?"

He shook his head. *Keep it together.*

"I suppose it *is* scary when the police know your movements," she said. "Because all that's left really is for you to admit what you've done. Did Bert fiddle with you? Is that what this is all about? Did you get angry? Lash out? What's the game grid? What does it mean to you?"

Zac winced.

'Come here, Zac, and suck my toe.'

"Fuck off," he snarled in The Voice of Fear.

"What did all those people do to you?" She sighed. "The worst bit of all is what you may have done with Kitty before you killed her..."

"No, I didn't do anything like *that*."

"Like what? I have no idea what you thought I was implying. But you saying what you have, thank you for that."

What had he just said? His mind was scrambled, and he couldn't remember.

"*What* did you do to her if it wasn't *that*?" Smith asked.

Oh God. He'd said more than he should. Something had slipped out, and he hadn't even noticed. "I didn't do anything to her like Bert did to me." *You gobby bastard! Shut your trap!*

"But you killed her, didn't you?" She stepped closer. "*Didn't. You?*"

Christ. Oh God... I can't think straight. "She saw me. I had to. She..." His head snapped back in the game. "I haven't done whatever it is you think I have."

But it was too late. By her face, he'd admitted something he shouldn't have.

"We know it was you," she said. "Killing all those people. I'm just curious as to who you are. Chicken or gorilla?"

He struggled to get Wilkins and that copper to loosen their grip.

"And that gun. If we get a warrant, are we going to find it in your house? It's foreign, so we'll know whether it was used to scare those victims."

"It's a fucking toy!" he shouted. *Shut up!*

She smiled, just briefly, then gave him a look of such hate he knew he'd reached the end of the road. Why had he blabbed? Why couldn't he control his mouth?

Smith stared at the sky for a moment, as if looking at Heaven. Then she glared at him again. "Zac Ferguson, I am arresting you for the murders of..."

That anger of his surged, and he fought the coppers' hold, the rest of what she said fading until...

"Jambrea Gaff..."

"That wasn't me. But it was *supposed* to be me," he shouted.

"Ian Stellar..."

"Fuck off. Fuck you! He wasn't mine either!"

And, too late, he realised what he'd done. If Jambrea and Stellar weren't his, by keeping quiet on the rest of the names, he'd admitted the others were.

"...it may harm your defence if you do not mention when questioned something which you later rely on in court. Anything you do say may be given in evidence."

He slumped, out of breath, out of fight.

It was over.

CHAPTER TWENTY-THREE

Bethany had left Zac in a holding cell while she and Mike had visited the next of kins for the Animal Gang members. Now, two hours later, she sat in the interview room, and her heart hurt, despite her attempt at hardening it. Zac had told his story, and while it in no way excused what he'd done, she understood how a mind got twisted and people acted in horrendous ways. He'd admitted to murdering everyone except Jambrea and Ian, and she accepted that. After all, they'd been aware two killers were in play, so who was the other one?

They hadn't had any joy tracking the red car.

She stared at him across the table. "Do you think someone just copied your kill method, is that it?"

Mike scribbled notes beside her. Talitia stood beside the door. Zac's solicitor sat next to him. He'd advised Zac to go 'no comment', but thankfully, Zac had declined that option.

"I swear to you, I don't know who it was, but it wasn't me."

She thought about the squat, the music floating out into the street. Shaggy. She almost blurted out more words to that song, about being caught red-handed, but *she* declined, too. "I actually believe you on that."

His eyebrows lifted. "You're not messing with me, are you?"

"No. We suspected a second killer. Why choose Susan Burrow over Ian Stellar, though? I don't understand that. Stellar posed the bigger threat. You said he'd basically told you he knew the Animal Gang had robbed him."

"He'd gone quiet because of Clancy. She shagged him to keep his mouth shut."

Was that why Ian had had a regular appointment with the other sex worker? He'd had a taste of Clancy, and when that ended, he'd picked someone else?

"So Susan Burrow literally just annoyed you? Because of the large fine?"

He shrugged.

"Kitty Longshaw." She sighed. Recalled looking up to Heaven and silently telling that little girl she was about to arrest the nasty man who'd killed her. "Why? Why couldn't you have just left her alone?"

"I would have, but I saw her again. And she recognised me."

"But don't you see, she only recognised you because you *followed* her and *let* her see you. At her age, she'd have forgotten you in a few weeks' time. And is it likely you'd even have been near that estate for her to spot you in the future?"

"No."

"Where did the large sum of money come from in your safe? The one in the wardrobe?"

He jolted at that. "You've been in my *house*?"

"Of course. We have a warrant."

"I don't want to talk about the money."

"Okay. What about the ticks?" Her stomach churned at the thought. She hadn't seen it, but Isabelle had let her know the damn things were stuck to a blackboard, and he'd drawn a chalk grid on it. "Why did you keep them?"

"Dunno."

"Let's talk about the Animal Gang. Why did you wait so long to kill them? That goes for everyone, really, apart from Kitty and Susan."

"I'd been thinking about it for years. Then Susan pissed me off, and that was it, I started planning. Thought of everyone who'd upset me. Can't explain it. I just had to do it."

"Who does the number belong to in your phone, the one you have down as 'date'? We've looked into it, and it's a burner, no longer in use. Do you have an accomplice? Is that who killed Jambrea and Stellar?"

"No comment."

Ah, so that might be the case. He was willing to protect someone. But why? He'd been treated unfairly throughout his life, if she was meant to believe his story, so who would he want to keep safe? He hadn't mentioned anyone other than the people he'd killed, Stellar, the Animal Gang, his parents—who he despised for allowing Bert into their home—the old lady in the shop during the robbery, plus the mother and her children.

"Okay, we'll leave it here," she said. "You need a break. Some food. A bit of rest. We'll continue tomorrow morning."

"What else is there to say? I told you who I killed. What does it matter why I did it? The person on my phone, you don't even need to know who it is. They're nothing to do with this. It's just someone I'd rather not mention."

"All right. Like I said, you need a break. Interview suspended at..."

"Fancy going for a drink, you lot?" Bethany asked the team. "I'll shout for the first round."

Mike, Fran, Leona, and Talitia gave various responses, all positive and jolly, and shut down their computers. Bethany didn't usually hang around with them after hours, apart from Mike, but she didn't want to go home alone, and a bit of a laugh with everyone was welcome.

They arranged to go to The Grubby—sadly, Bethany couldn't stop herself from wanting to see if Evan Crow was in. He'd been distraught when told his brother had been killed because he'd tried to stop a member of a gang after the Stellar robbery. He was alone, no one to call his own anymore, and she related to that.

Bethany arranged for two taxis, and at the pub, they all bundled out, a sense of excitement buzzing off everyone. They'd caught a warped killer who at the same time seemed so normal, and a celebration was in order. Her offer of paying for the first round was for a job well done.

Inside, they lined the bar, Fran mentioning she'd only be staying for one so she could get home and bake butterfly cakes with her little one before bed, something she'd promised this morning as she'd flown out of the house for work. Drinks poured, they each carried them to a table in the corner, by a woman and a man, who had their heads bent and talked low.

Evan appeared, and he approached the bar. He nodded to her then turned away, making it clear he didn't want to chat. She'd have to respect that, no matter how much she wanted to offer him some comforting words.

While her team nattered away, Bethany caught a foreign accent coming from the lady nearby. She glanced at her—black hair, thick-lens glasses, lurid makeup, a hideous cerise blouse, fake silk, shiny.

"Then it is agreed," she said. "You will leave the rest in the designated place. Now we must go to the toilet."

Where had she heard that accent before?

"Oi, Beth, did you just hear what Leona said?" Fran, her eyes bright, had laughter in her voice.

Bethany gave them her attention, and with Leona's tale retold, Bethany chuckled, so pleased she had this team. She really needed to do this more often, get out into the world, live for more than just her job and her promise to Vinny to throw herself into work so she didn't feel alone.

It felt good to be with them, her friends and family all rolled into one, and she swallowed the lump in her throat. Despite being without her husband, she was so lucky.

Erica rushed out of The Grubby, her heart rate still spiking from when she'd recognised two of the coppers who'd been at Zac's earlier—the man who'd opened the door and the young woman who'd stood outside by the hedge. Maybe she should use a different pub for each client. Okay, she had her disguise on, but her voice gave her away.

She drove home, her next job secure, the first half of the payment in her bag, and now she'd have to pack for the holiday Lenny had paid for with his guest money. He'd better not annoy her while they were away. She couldn't be doing with strangling him in unfamiliar territory.

She parked up on her drive and removed the wig, the glasses, and cleaned off the makeup. Went inside. Stood at the living room door. Lenny had his phone out. Lenny had something else out, too, poking out of his pants.

Yes, she'd *so* be killing him.

Dirty little piglet.

Made in the USA
San Bernardino, CA
09 March 2020